GRAVEYARD SHIFT *at the* LEMONADE STAND

stories

TIM BOWLING

. . .

GRAVEYARD SHIFT *at the* LEMONADE STAND

Freehand Books gratefully acknowledges the financial support for its publishing program provided by the Canada Council for the Arts and the Alberta Media Fund, and by the Government of Canada through the Canada Book Fund.

This book is available in print and Global Certified Accessible™ epub formats.

Freehand Books is located in Moh'kinsstis, Calgary, Alberta, within Treaty 7 territory, and on the traditional territories of the Siksika, the Kainai, and the Piikani, as well as the Iyarhe Nakoda and Tsuut'ina nations.

LIBRARY AND ARCHIVES CANADA CATALOGUING IN PUBLICATION
Title: Graveyard shift at the lemonade stand : stories / Tim Bowling.
Names: Bowling, Tim, 1964– author.
Identifiers:
Canadiana (print) 20240519574
Canadiana (ebook) 20240519582
ISBN 9781990601866 (softcover)
ISBN 9781990601873 (EPUB)
ISBN 9781990601880 (PDF)
Subjects: LCGFT: Short stories.
Classification: LCC PS8553.O9044 | G73 2025 | DDC C813/.54—dc23

Edited by Deborah Willis
Design by Peter Cocking
Cover photo by shaunl/iStock
Printed and bound in Canada

FIRST PRINTING

FREEHAND BOOKS
freehand-books.com

Canada | Canada Council for the Arts / Conseil des arts du Canada | Alberta Government *for Dashiell, Sadie, and Levi*

. . .

Contents

. . .

The Living

. . .

IT IS MONDAY and so, when the rain starts, almost immediately I hear the squeaking of the pulleys of the laundry lines all along our street. There's nothing else to hear, except Pepper's breathing and the faint-loud-faint-loud hum of a bumblebee over me where I lie in the tall grass. Without getting up and looking, I can see Mrs. Klassen and Mrs. Lord and my mother standing on their respective back porches with wooden clothes pegs between their lips as the bleached bedsheets darken and become like the big wall maps in my classroom at school.

Finally, the rain stops, and I stand as if summoned. At first, the neighbourhood's a sea-swell falling away to the horizon. I touch the feathery top of Pepper's head to steady myself. Together we watch the two men come down off the dyke, my father in gumboots so black he might have been standing up to his knees in tar, the stranger hunched sideways just like the picture of Atlas holding the earth that I found in a book of myths I once took out from the library.

The sun, low in the sky, cracks red through the massed black cloud. Pepper wags his tail and starts forward. Then, abruptly, he stops and growls, inching back, as my father and the stranger approach along the grey pavement darkened with oil splatters and tire-crushed cherries dropped from the beaks of crows and starlings. I hold Pepper by the collar and watch until the two men stop, directly under the bloody gash in the sky, and my father calls me over. Now Pepper's teeth are fully bared and it takes all my strength to hold him as I do a sort of stutter-step out of the grass and onto the road. Finally, I lose my grip and Pepper lunges forward, barking and barking. My father shouts at him to stop and then orders him away.

All this time, the stranger does not speak. His right, thick-knuckled hand twitches at the belt loop of his baggy pants, as if he's searching for the missing belt. I look up into his wrinkled face. He has a broad nose lined with broken blood vessels, grey stubble on his cheeks, and squinting eyes the size of cherry pits. This man smells of wet earth and mulch. It's a smell powerful enough to cover the heavy musk of salmon that flows off my father's mackinaw and the dead jack spring he holds by the gill in one hand, the burlap sack of sockeye he holds in the other.

"Catchin' flies, son?" The stranger grins, his tongue a thick wad of grey between his teeth.

I quickly close my mouth and look down.

My father chuckles and double clutches the burlap sack. "Danny, this is Mr. Johnson. He's from the States."

"Oh jes call me Jim. Mr.'s too fine a word for these sorry old bones."

I decide right away not to call the man anything. I'll just talk to him respectfully if I have to talk to him at all. We almost never have strangers to the house, rarely have visitors at all except for family. Right now, my mother's older sister has come from Toronto for a two-week vacation. Auntie Muriel wears her grey hair in a severe bun and is always sucking air through her teeth. Her eyes are black and small, like a salmon's, and, also like a salmon's, they never close but peer out with an unsettling intensity. But she's nice to me and sometimes gives me quarters to buy candy. Her husband died many years ago and she has no children of her own, so I think it makes her happy to buy me treats. I wonder whether she might even give me some money today; I'd like to buy some caramels or banana mojos. But it's getting late, and I probably won't be allowed to walk to the store, even though it's summer and the height of the fishing season and we're not keeping regular hours as we do when school starts and the river closes and the leaves on the big maple in our front yard blaze gold and red.

"Jim here," my father says with an awe in his voice that he generally reserves for the animal kingdom, "is a travelling man."

"Like Tommy Hunter," I say, thinking of the song from my father's favourite TV show. *I'm a travelling man, travelling the breeze, travelling here, travelling there, gathering memories. So let me wander, let me wander…*

My father smiles and swings the little jack spring like a dim lantern. Blood drips off the fanned tail and leaves a vivid splotch on the pavement. "No, not exactly, Dan." He sounds embarrassed. "There's a difference between TV and real living."

The stranger sighs. "That's so. You listen to yore daddy, son. I been on the road pretty near all my life and they ain't nothing neat and tidy about it that you can put inside one of them little picture boxes."

"Jim's from Mississippi. He used to work on the steamboats."

"Oh now, that's going back some. Ancient history. But I remember it like it was jes yestidday. Yes sir, I can see that big old muddy river and them boats all lit up like birthday cakes with the fine folks and the cardsharps and what all having a gay old time of it. Except when they was fightin' instead. If you was a tad older, son, there's tales I could tell you, shore."

The man's left shoulder is perhaps two or three inches lower than his right and even his voice slides off to one side.

"Well." My father swings the fish away from his leg again. "Come on to the house, Jim. We'll have a quick bite to eat before we head out for the dark set."

My mouth drops open once more. Never in my life have I known my father to take someone fishing who isn't family. There's something wrong about it, as if my father had suddenly decided to throw all the fish he had caught back into the river. I watch him and the stranger walk down the driveway and up the four wooden stairs to our house. Pepper's barking fills the air once more and finally makes me follow, if only to comfort him.

The red in the sky broadens and thins and the air is cooler. It hangs from the dusk like a bedsheet on the laundry line left out in the rain. By the time I push through it and enter the house, Jim is politely refusing the whole of my parents' hospitality.

"No, thank you, ma'am. If it's all the same to you, I'd prefer to sleep outdoors and take my meals there too. I don't aim to put anyone out. It's not my way, you see."

"Meals, is it?" Arms crossed over her chest, a scowl fixed on her lean face, Auntie Muriel stands beside my mother at the stove. They might be two little girls in a playground again, the older protecting the younger.

The stranger ducks his head slightly. He turns and touches the doorknob. "The good Lord made the great outdoors for the first man and I reckon what's good enough for Adam is plenty good enough for Jim Johnson."

"We'll just serve you there, then?"

"Muriel!" My mother's blush spreads quickly.

My father coughs and gently lays a hand on the stranger's low shoulder. "I'll eat with you, Jim. Vi, we must have some extra blankets at least. It'll be cold in the morning when we get in."

My father turns and sees me standing in the open doorway. "Dan can bring the supper out for us. I'll get a fire going."

As soon as the door closes, my aunt starts sucking air through her teeth as if she's got a candy stuck in place of her molars.

"It's a good thing," she says finally, "that he's not planning on staying in the house. It's bad enough to let him stay in the yard. I've a good mind to go into town and rent a hotel room and take the child with me." She takes a wooden spoon off the counter and stirs something on the stove. The scent of onions fills the kitchen.

"He seems a gentle sort," my mother says.

"You can bet your bottom dollar that he isn't. I suppose you don't get many tramps like that around here. The city's full of them. Mark my words. Just give that fellow an inch and… "

My mother raises an eyebrow and I know that she's reminding Auntie Muriel of my presence. But I've heard enough to know that my aunt is as instinctively suspicious as I am.

Thick steam rises from the kettle. My mother pours the boiled water into two tea mugs and tells me to carry them carefully into the yard.

"I'll call you to come and get the supper. It won't be too long. Now, Muriel, we have to get to these fish."

The burlap sack my father had carried lies on the linoleum, a sockeye's head sticking out, one black eye gazing up at the ceiling. The smell of slime and blood and river muffles the onion fumes.

My aunt bends to the sack and hooks the visible salmon under the gill. Though she has lived in Toronto most of her life, Auntie Muriel is comfortable with country ways and always plans her visits to us when she can be of the most use with all the canning that goes on towards the end of summer and the beginning of fall. And my mother, who is still a little squeamish when she has to reach in and remove the windpipe from a plucked pheasant, is grateful for the help. She says that Auntie Muriel lived through the Depression as a teenaged girl in a large family and that that sort of experience teaches resourcefulness.

Now the two sisters begin to clean the salmon and there's a scraping of scales with a knife edge and my aunt's low mutter expressing again and again her unhappiness with the tramp's appearance. "Old as he is, still roaming around, you can just bet he's trouble . . . "

As soon as I step outside, I can hear the crack of twigs down the dark lane to the backyard. My father's building a fire in the brick pit, carefully constructing a pyramid before he adds the chunks of bark he's caught in his net and brought home and dried for days in the sun. Through the summer and fall, we have fires almost every night, sitting for hours, watching satellites cross slowly through the constellations as we drink mugs of sweet tea and roast marshmallows and wieners on long twigs broken off the cherry tree. I love to be alone with my parents then, and with my father once my mother goes back inside. Usually I don't say much, just listen to them talk about their day, or other people in the town, or something that happened years ago, usually to a family member. Sometimes, discreetly, they discuss my older brothers, both of whom are also fishermen, away for the summer on seine boats. I know that my mother fears that they drink too much and that my father is less concerned. He's an easygoing parent, even to me, though I am, as he sometimes jokes, a special child, the child of his autumn years. And it's true; my parents are old enough to be my grandparents and perhaps that is why we're so comfortable together, not even having to speak much, just sitting together sipping tea and watching the embers die down as the bats flit through the smoky darkness overhead.

But this night is different. The stranger has taken the wooden lawn chair in which my mother normally sits and is drawing deeply on one of my father's cigarettes while my father, squatting, tends the fire. As I come closer, I hear the tramp telling a story about something that happened to him when he was a boy on one of the Mississippi steamboats, and before I have listened for even thirty seconds I recognise the story from another book I have taken out of the library. The recognition confuses me. I stand just outside the warmth that begins to crackle and reach into the descending dusk and try to understand why the stranger is telling my father a story from a book as if it was something that really happened to him. Neither of my parents reads books and so I'm not surprised that my father laughs as if the story is actually the stranger's own. And the tramp is very good at the telling. After a while, I even forget my confusion and begin to enjoy the story all over again, which is somehow better in the tramp's deep drawl punctuated with chuckles and broken grins and one hand slapping his thigh.

Then, before I know it, my mother's whistling from the doorway for me to come and get the supper and I have to turn away into the thicker and colder dusk. Moments later, when I return, with more of my aunt's discontent clouding my perception, the fire's growth seems a kind of violence that has taken the place of the tramp. In the crackle and blaze of it, he's gone silent, almost motionless but for the steady twitching of one hand. I look more carefully at him in the crisscross of flickers. He is very old, his face more cracked than wrinkled, as if gouged out by constant, cold winds. His chest is sunken, the shoulders bony, his flannel shirt mis-buttoned so that it hangs as unevenly as his frame. Leaning back in the chair, his unblinking face lifted a little towards the slowly deepening stars, he is hardly more present than the smoke curling into the plum-black dark. And yet there is my aunt's concern and the tramp's own storytelling, which isn't exactly a lie but which I know is false in some important way. And then there is also my father's voice, explaining that they should eat quickly and get back to the boat before it's completely dark, so that he can set his net across the water just at that time when the salmon are less able to see the meshes. It is the tramp's easy positioning in my father's almost hermetic world that disturbs me most, and as I go back to the house, unthanked, unnoticed even, I know that I do not want the tramp's tired voice and mismatched stance to remain any longer than necessary.

In the morning I wake early to the sound of low voices coming through my open bedroom window. My father says, "Are you sure you won't come into the house, we have plenty of room," and there's a softer response that I can't make out, followed by my father again, insisting that he'll build a fire to keep the worst of the chill away. I climb out of bed and stand at the window. The air is cool, heavy with the musk of river-mud and brine and the first hints of rotting windfall under the pear tree between the house and the backyard. It is closer to day than night now, even though the air is grainy with remnants of dark. I know my father would have remained on the river to make the daybreak set if the fishing had been good, and somehow the idea of a bad night of fishing goes naturally with the tramp's unwanted presence. Already I'm convinced that he's bad luck, that the fishing won't improve until he's gone. I climb back into bed and eventually doze for a few more minutes until the smoke from the fire wakes me.

Before I enter the kitchen, I hear my parents and aunt talking and so I decide to remain in the hallway and listen. There's a slight sizzling sound and the enticing aroma of fried potatoes and I have to force myself not to walk right out and ask for my breakfast.

"He's harmless," my father says. "What else could he be at his age? But I doubt he was ever anything else anyway. Just because a man likes to move around doesn't make him dangerous."

My aunt sucks air through her teeth but says nothing.

"It made for a pleasant night at least." My father yawns. "Helped pass the time. His stories, I mean. You know, I don't think there's a state he hasn't been to, except maybe Hawaii. Imagine that."

Even though I can't see her, I know the sharp scowl has settled on my aunt's face when she says, "Maybe he wasn't allowed to stay in one place, maybe he had no choice."

"Oh for crying out loud."

"Frank."

My father's voice drops. "Well, it isn't fair to judge a man as quick as all that."

"He's an old tramp," my aunt says. "And nobody gets that way without being trouble. You mark my words..."

"How about you both eat your breakfast?" my mother says, and there's a small clatter of plates. "Danny'll be getting up soon and I don't want him thinking there's anything to worry about."

"Forewarned is forearmed," my aunt says.

"He's eight, Muriel." My mother sighs. "I don't want him armed at all just yet."

When the silence descends for several seconds and my father begins to talk about a snag that tore a large hole in his net, I realise it's safe for me to appear. On emerging, I'm greeted with the usual enthusiasm, though I am aware that all three adults are studying me with more intensity than usual. It is not a comfortable feeling, as too much study generally means less freedom. And I plan to collect beer bottles along the riverbank at low tide today. Already the stranger has become a threat to me.

So when my mother asks me to take a mug of tea out to the yard for him, I'm not pleased at the prospect.

"If he's sleeping," she says, "don't disturb him. I'll make him a fresh mug later."

"If he is asleep," my father adds, "put another chunk of bark on the fire. But quietly, okay?"

My aunt pushes her chair back with a loud scrape. "Honestly. You'd think he was the Prince of Wales."

My father winks at me. "Maybe he is. He could be in disguise, you never know."

When I step outside, I immediately notice that something's wrong. I can smell the straw and wet fur coming off the doghouse but Pepper's not there. I call for him and the door behind me opens and my mother says, "Shhh. Dad put Pepper in the storage room, it's all right. He kept growling at Jim."

This is too much. I can hardly find the words to express my outrage. At last they come tumbling out. "But Pepper lives here. He's family."

"It's only for the morning. So Jim can get some rest. Remember, Danny, don't wake him. Just bring the tea back if he's asleep."

But not only is the tramp not sleeping, he's not even lying down. He's sitting in my mother's chair, pulled up close to the fire, and he's cracking peanut shells and eating the peanuts. The shells are scattered all around his worn boots and there's little flecks of the peanut skin stuck to his lips. To my annoyance, I see that he's wearing one of my father's down-filled hunting jackets and is wiping his greasy hands on the fabric in between cracking peanuts. When he notices me, the tramp smiles, but it isn't exactly friendly.

"It's nice to have a servant," he says. "Even if it's just a kid."

I put the mug of tea into his reaching hands, which are gloved but only up to the knuckles. He takes a long sip, then licks his lips and squints at me.

"Don't worry. Your aunt isn't any happier than you are that I'm here. She'll get me out. Or else I don't know that type. Soon as she smells a free man, a woman like that is a dog on a gristly bone."

He pauses, takes another sip of tea, then nods.

"Ah, you're mad about your dog? I don't blame you. I'd be mad too. But dogs are like women; they don't like what they can't predict. You ever wonder why dogs hate cats so much? Because they can't be sure whether a cat's going to run or stay and scratch their eyeballs out."

The tramp puts the mug on the arm of the chair, then cracks another peanut shell. The fire's warmth holds me in place long enough for the realisation to strike: his accent is gone. I stare at him, my eyes unblinking.

He chuckles and balances half of a peanut shell on two fingertips. I look away and watch a honeybee crawl around the sweet rim of his mug.

In a parody of accent, he says, "Why, you shore is a bright chile, like yore daddy done tole me. A big book reader. Ain't dat so?"

He lifts the open half shell closer to his face. Without looking at me, he says "You're smart, but you're just a kid. It isn't you I have to worry about. And it isn't your father or even your mother. But that aunt; I've met the likes of her before. Yeah, I'll get a few meals at most." Now he fixes me with a double squint and there's neither warmth nor coldness in his voice. "Huck Finn and Tom Sawyer. They say it's a kids' book, only they never say why. But you're smart, you've already read it, so I'll tell you. Because every man makes a choice. You'll make it too. Are you going to grow up and be a man? Are you going to light out? That's it, kid. That's all. Are you going to light out?"

He puts his left hand out to the mug and notices the bee. Without even pausing, he scoops it into his hand and makes a tight fist and holds it awhile. Then he opens his palm. The bee lies twitching on the soiled wool of his glove. The tramp brings his other hand over and places the peanut shell on the arm of the chair.

"Lighting out. It means you can get stung and you don't even feel it. That's what a man needs. And you can only get it the way a bee gets honey. By moving." He stares at the little corpse in his hand. "Then you get slow and the moving's over." He takes the bee between two fingers and places it neatly inside the half shell. Then he finds another half shell at his feet and fits it to the first. "Here, kid. You keep it. And if you don't say anything to your folks about our little talk, I promise I'll be gone before your dog barks itself to death."

I look at the peanut shell in my hand. I can hardly believe that there's a dead bee inside, even though the tramp has just put it there. After all, it isn't something an adult does. When I turn my gaze onto him, the event seems even more impossible, for he's just leaning back in the chair, sipping tea. When he realises that I'm staring at him, he says, "I'll likely move on tonight after a good supper. But you can't say anything before then. Got it?"

Three days later, however, he hasn't moved on. In fact, he shows no signs of doing so, even though he makes a point of telling me at least twice a day that he'll leave soon but only if I promise not to say anything about our little talk. I'm not sure what to do. I don't like having him around; he monopolises my father's company and upsets my aunt and restricts Pepper's freedom. But every time I think of telling my parents about his deceitfulness, somehow the dead bee in its peanut shell comes into my mind; it's as if my telling might wake the bee and cause it to chase after me with its stinger, a kind of Snow-White story in reverse. And yet, curiously, I keep the peanut shell on my bedroom windowsill and look at it every night before going to sleep. I can't bring myself to look at the bee, however. And the more time that passes, the more I'm convinced that what I would find inside the shell would be terrible. Even worse, the tramp seems to know all about my fear. He squints at me when my parents and aunt aren't around and says, "I wonder how that little bee's doing now."

Gradually, my aunt's displeasure starts to influence my mother. She doesn't complain openly about the tramp's extended stay, but she shows less concern for his welfare and asks fewer questions about him. Instead, she makes regular, pointed references to the fishing season, to the lack of success my father has had ever since the tramp's arrival. I know that my mother is superstitious, that she doesn't like me to step on cracks in the sidewalk or to cut my fingernails on a Sunday, and I guess that, with my aunt's help, she has begun to see the tramp as an albatross. I realise it's only a matter of time before things come to a head.

I have just returned home from school, wandering slowly in the mellow, mid-September sunlight, not exactly eager to see how much deeper my father has fallen under the stranger's spell. The two have become inseparable. When they aren't on the boat together, they sit in the backyard, having big fires no matter the time of day, the tramp talking and my father smiling and nodding his head and asking questions about the Mississippi and how it compares with the Fraser. I'm both embarrassed for him and angered by the tramp's deceit. Day by day, hour by hour, their two bodies are blending in the steady fireglow; the tramp wears my father's clothes, drinks his tea, smokes his cigarettes, and eats his meals. And as soon as my father accepts some peanuts from the tramp's gloved hand, the merging is complete. Or it would be, it would lead perhaps to my father going out late to the fishing grounds or not going out at all, as my aunt predicts in fierce whispers to my mother, if not for what happens this particular afternoon.

As soon as I step into the kitchen, my mother confronts me.

"Danny, did you take any money from the jar?"

I shake my head vigorously while my aunt makes tutting noises, directed, I realise, at my mother for her lack of faith in me.

My mother sighs. "Do you swear, Danny, that you didn't?"

"Violet, for heaven sakes, you know he didn't."

I swear again to my innocence, but my mother shows no relief at my position. She just puts the empty mason jar back in the cupboard above the sink and faces my aunt, who is almost grinning out of her iron disapproval. Suddenly I understand why. In fact, I understand too well. I stare at Auntie Muriel, hardly able to accept what my instincts have just told me.

"It could have been anyone," my mother says. "Anyone could just walk in off the street."

But I know that she puts no faith in her words. If she did, she would consider the word "anyone" more carefully. Instead, she unties her apron and folds it neatly on the counter before slipping her cardigan over her shoulders and walking to the door.

"I'm coming with you," my aunt says. "There's no telling what he'll do."

I know they don't want me to come, so I take off my jacket and head into the living room. As soon as they step outside, however, I leave the house by the back door and follow. As I expect, my mother and aunt are too intent on their mission to notice me.

From twenty feet away I watch as my mother leans down to my father and he stands and walks back with her away from the fire. The tramp turns his head slightly, then cracks a peanut shell. I have a powerful impression that it's his head that has cracked, as if it's inside the fire. I begin to tremble as my father's voice reaches me.

"That's nonsense. Maybe you took it and forgot."

"When have I ever forgotten something like that?"

"Well, what do you want me to do?"

"I want you to get it back. I need it for groceries."

At this point, my aunt steps closer. "We've been feeding one more than usual."

My father raises his voice. "Two, actually."

My aunt makes no effort to keep her voice low. "I would think family is different. But if I have to pay for my room and board, I will."

"If you don't get it back," my mother almost hisses, "I'll have to do it."

"Jesus H. Christ." My father's neck has become corrugated iron. "All right. But I'm telling you right now, you're both wrong. He's no thief."

All this time the tramp just keeps cracking peanut shells and tossing them into the fire. The sunlight dapples his tilted shoulders. I catch a strong whiff of rotting pear out of the smoke, which somehow seems to burn right off the tramp's body. He's burning and I can't stop trembling. I hate him. I want him to turn to ash and blow away over the fence and sink into the tide and be washed away forever.

But he remains in my mother's chair as my father comes back and takes up his fire-stick and pokes at the logs. I hide from my mother and aunt as they pass, but I know my time is limited. Soon my mother will realise that I'm not in the house and she'll come looking for me. I creep closer to the fire.

For a long minute there's only the sound of crackling logs and cracking peanut shells. I hate the tramp even more for not helping my father, for not making this easier for him. Of course, I know that the tramp didn't steal the money, but he's a thief anyway. So what difference does it make what kind of thief he is? Slowly I begin to lose patience with my father. He has to choose, just as the tramp himself had said. So why doesn't he? After all, the choice is simple.

My father lights a cigarette and takes a long drag. Then he passes the cigarette to the tramp, who takes his own drag but does not give the cigarette back. I look towards the house. I can almost feel the door opening, feel my mother's voice calling me to her. And still my father does not mention the money. Finally, I can stand it no longer.

"I saw him take it," I say, and step into the fire's warmth.

My father's head snaps up while the tramp's turns slowly, as if on a spit. I struggle to keep the two heads separate, but I'm aware only of the eyes, and they are not my father's. And it isn't that I see them or even feel them; it's stranger than that, more as if I'm looking at myself from a great distance. I wrench myself back to my father, whose face is suddenly worn, his eyes bloodshot.

"You're sure, Dan? This isn't something to joke about."

I realise that he has to say these things, even though we all know that they're false. Joking is the last thing that anybody would think of; even the tramp, when he killed the bee and coffined it and asked me how it was doing, did not intend a joke. In fact, it's the absence of humour, the shrinking of its presence in our house and lives, that scares me above all else.

I nod and my father does the same. He pushes his stick into the burning logs and there's a low whoosh as a part of the fire collapses in on itself.

"Jim," he says. "We're missing some money from the house. My boy here says he saw you take it."

Now the tramp surprises me. He doesn't defend himself, nor does he look at me in anger. He grins, and his whole face seems to explode with life. All the wan firelight and heavy sunlight rush to frame his wrinkled features. His teeth are large and blunt and shockingly white. Just as I think he's going to laugh a terrible, tear-infected laugh, he makes no sound for several seconds.

My father lowers his eyes to the fire. The quick rhythm of a chickadee's song drips out of the day beyond us. I'm painfully aware of the thick smoke in my nostrils but I can't turn away from the tramp's grim beatitude. He appears to rise from his chair even as his bones, muscles, and flesh gain solidity.

At last, he speaks in a tone of thrilled evenness that's much worse than hatred or scorn.

"So, you lit out, kid? It's early for you, but some know early. Some just know. But it isn't the knowing, it's the living with it."

I look at my father to see how he's taking the tramp's vanished accent. But he just pokes at the fire again and sends a wreathed bit of black ash skyward.

The tramp stands slowly and brushes a few peanut shells off his chest.

"You know I didn't take it, so you know I can't give it back. The best I can do for you is to leave."

My father nods but his head seems cast-iron; he can't keep it lifted long enough to meet the tramp's eyes.

"Keep the jacket," my father says. Then, after a pause, he adds, "Where will you go now?"

The tramp looks at me as he responds. "The next place. Nowhere else *to* go." He thanks my father for his hospitality, accepts a package of cigarettes for the road, and walks past me without even a glance.

In the long, crackling silence after his departure, my father doesn't move, nor does he look at me. He gazes into the fire and pokes the bark. More ash, black and urgent and ragged as the salmon's gaze, drifts skyward and dissolves.

"He did take it," I say weakly, hating myself for the smallness of the lie, hating my father for accepting the smallness without rage, without any discernible response at all. Lost, weak in the legs, I step over to the chair the tramp has left empty. A peanut shell cracks under my foot and his words rise out of the sound: "It isn't the knowing, it's the living with it." I hear them over and over, until I have entombed them in the shell with the dead bee, for a safekeeping that is never safe and has no end, I hear them again now, across the decades and the graves of my parents and my aunt, and I hear them in the brittle past of windowsills and windfall and eyes that never close as the daylight drains away, the dusk heaves in, and the fire deepens at the end of my father's reach.

Kapelznik in the Bottom of the Ninth

. . .

WITH THE bases loaded, two outs, and a run down. It happens in baseball, at all levels, all the time, more than you'd think. From Little League to the pros, somebody's always driving in the game-winning runs or striking out in this situation. And the funny thing is, it's almost always a hit or a strikeout, rarely a routine pop-up or a groundout or a base on balls.

Bobby Kapelznik probably wasn't thinking about statistics, but I'm sure he was feeling every bit of their influence as he stood there sweating in the ninety-degree heat, with maybe forty pairs of eyes focused on him. To be honest, I didn't know what he was thinking about. As his coach, I was hoping he'd be thinking, "Wait for my pitch, just make good contact, take a level swing, eyes on the ball." But as a man, I wouldn't have blamed him if he was thinking, "Throw the damned ball and get this over with," or "I'm just going to stand here and do nothing at all, not even when the game's over," or "Who gives a fuck about this shit?"

Because Bobby Kapelznik was twelve going on forty, and I'd never met a kid like him in over thirty years of coaching.

First of all, he was big. That's a polite way to put it. At five foot three or four, he weighed at least 170 pounds, and often it seemed that most of those pounds were on his shoulders. He had the most striking combination of moon-round white skin and giant freckles that it was humanly possible to have. Even at the height of August, when he stood at the plate with the South Delta Bronco Championship on the line, he had no tan – his face was just a little pink-tinged where the freckles, between the size of a ladybug and a thumb print, didn't show. And his lips – the poor kid – were thick and red and oddly moist, just as if he wore lipstick. You can imagine what other twelve-year-old boys made of that. But at least he had the self-protective instinct to wear his blond hair short – sure, the stubbly crewcut made his face balloon even larger, until you thought it was going to snap off his neck and float into the cumulous, but long hair with those lips would have been a death sentence. Well, not actual death – I mean the death of unrelenting persecution, which to a twelve-year-old kid might be worse than actual death. Sometimes it seems that way. Kapelznik would have had something interesting to say about that. Kapelznik, you see, had views.

The first day I met him, when I held the team's first practice, he arrived at the diamond differently than all the other kids. They biked or rode a skateboard; half of them were dropped off by their parents who immediately drove away. And then I saw this big kid climbing over the home run fence. He landed with an almost audible splat, then picked himself up like a sack of marshmallows and ambled over, hitching up his cut-off jeans and flapping his glove in front of him. It looked as if he was being attacked by a rabid bat, except that the glove, I noted with disbelief as he approached, was blue. Powder blue.

A collective groan went up amongst the other boys. That was all I needed to hear to know that this kid wasn't likely a great athlete in Fatty Arbuckle's body. And then one of the boys groaned, "Not Kapelznik," and I had a name to put to the grinning moon with owl eyes and no eyelashes.

"Hi Coach," he said, gasping. "Sorry I'm late."

I told him he wasn't late. Then one of the boys said, "You didn't walk from home, did you?"

Kapelznik shrugged. "Sure. I always walk. Walking's good for you. It's like the violin to the body."

Another collective groan, but I was curious.

"The violin?"

He punched the pocket of his glove as he responded. "Yeah, well, any instrument, really. But violin's the best. It fires your whole brain, all at once. Walking's like the violin for the body."

"Then why are you so fat?" somebody said, without malice.

Kapelznik looked genuinely puzzled by the question. "Genetics. And besides, I like to eat. And besides besides, I'm not fat. I'm like Obelix. You know, well-covered."

I couldn't help myself. "Obelix?"

"From *Asterix and Obelix*, the comic. You know, from Europe." Kapelznik finished working on his glove, and then blurted out, "What position do you want me to play, Coach?"

I took a deep breath. This kid was a surprising ball of energy, given his girth. "We'll get to that, Kapelz… uh, what's your first name?"

He gazed slowly upward. "What do you call somebody in the water with no arms and no legs?"

"Oh shut up, Kapelznik!"

The other kids all started to move away, picking up balls from my open duffel bag and beginning to toss them around. In the general bustle, I almost didn't hear Kapelznik's guffaw of an answer.

"Bob! It's a palindrome too."

And then he ambled away to try and find a throwing partner. When he failed, I accepted the job, still trying to remember what the hell a palindrome was.

Over the next few weeks, I learned that Kapelznik couldn't throw or field or bat very well, though every now and again, maybe one in twenty times, he clobbered a ball deep into the outfield. The problem was, he couldn't run very well either, and almost always got thrown out at first where the average kid would have had a stand-up double. I also learned that he had no friends, that when he walked from home, he walked several miles from one of the town's outlying farms, and that he had the most unorthodox patter in the league. The adults were clearly as irritated with him as the kids were.

"Come on, Curt, hit the eyes off that old spud!"

"Pitcher's got a prosthetic arm."

"Hum now, Brad boy, he couldn't hit you if you were Poland."

I spent much of the year trying to figure that last one out for myself, but I never could. It somehow made strange sense in the middle of a game, though. I came to like Kapelznik and to feel protective towards him. The kid just didn't get it. I mean, he had to know that he was odd and that revelling in it wasn't the best way to go. Yet he persisted. Maybe he figured he didn't stand a chance anyway, not with that body and that face. Somehow, I couldn't bring myself to ask him about it, or about much else, to be honest. I saw him only a few times a week, and I was running practice and games for fourteen other kids – there wasn't a lot of time to chat. And I had distractions too, of a personal nature.

Anyway, things would have been fine, the season would have come and gone like any other, except for one little problem: this group of boys was exceptionally talented, and, despite Kapelznik, they just kept winning. Before long, they had won the league, an invitational tournament in the city, and were poised to take the zone, which would lead to the Provincials and possibly the Nationals. I hardly had to coach them at all.

Except I did. And one thing that a good coach of children has to do is make sure that everybody plays. Everybody. It's not always simple, especially if the kids and their parents suddenly get heavily invested in the team's success. You have to find a balance, for everyone's sake, including the weaker kids. Sometimes they just want to go along for the ride, are happy to sit in the dugout and cheer as the wins pile up and the games become more important. But then maybe their parents aren't so happy, not understanding that their boy's greatest fear is that he'll be the goat. And then there are those weak players who genuinely want to play, and it becomes the coach's job to play them where they'll do the least damage – out in right field, late in the batting order, early in the game.

Kapelznik wasn't quite so easy to figure out. He loved to play. As bad as he could be – and I stopped counting his errors and strikeouts early in the season – he loved to play. In fact, I rarely saw that boy without a goofy grin on his face. But Kapelznik also loved to watch. He really got into it, the patter, organising the bats and helmets. I sometimes even let him coach first or third, if one of the insistent fathers wasn't around. And that's another point: Kapelznik's parents were completely absent. I never saw them, never heard from them, and he never said anything about them. So I had no pressure on that score. Ah, but the other parents: once we started to win so much that the Provincials were possible, *they* had opinions about whether Kapelznik should play or not. And that's when I got my back up. That's when I really let the boy down. Because I used him just the way I'd use a bunt squeeze in the ninth or a double steal; I used him just to show everyone who was boss. Naturally enough, I screwed things up, to the point where Kapelznik, batting in the bottom of the ninth with two outs, bases loaded, a run down, meant the difference between going to the Provincials or going home. I served that boy up like a lamb to the wolves and there was nothing I could do but watch the pack close in.

. . .

IT HADN'T BEEN a good summer for me, apart from on the ball diamond. My wife and I had split after twenty-five years of marriage, and our two boys – twenty and eighteen – weren't happy about it. They blamed me. Even though their mother explained the situation as it really was – that we simply no longer enjoyed each other's company, and that neither of us was happy – they still blamed me. After all, I was the coach; I'd been their coach all through their childhoods; I was the one giving the signals from the dugout. Well, I couldn't do anything except soak up their blame and wait for their acceptance of reality. As for mine: I lived in a crummy bachelor apartment whose floor was covered in takeout food bags and dirty clothes and empties and tried to figure out ways to keep my relationship with my sons as healthy as possible. It was tough. And often, through that summer, all that kept me going was the baseball coaching. It was a distraction I came to depend on.

But somehow, I still lost sight of Kapelznik. Those goddamned parents of the gifted boys, those doctors and lawyers and whatever else with their A-type personalities and their hunger to have their kids succeed, blinded me. I had to beat them, I had to win that game, probably because I had lost my marriage and was losing my boys, or maybe just because I was tired of the bullshit that goes along with kids' sports. It doesn't really matter why, but I somehow put Kapelznik right in the crosshairs – that fat, goofy kid with the funny mouth and weird comments, who walked all the way from the farm to play ball with kids who didn't want him around, who made that walk – and Jesus, I *knew* this, I just wasn't paying attention; because he was lonely, as plain as that, and he didn't know any other ways to deal with it except to keep putting himself in places where his loneliness might just be set in stone forever. And if you think that's an exaggeration, you don't know childhood, you don't know the first thing about it.

"Listen, Charlton," the star pitcher's hawk-faced father hissed through the wire fencing of the dugout just after we'd loaded the bases and everyone's eyes zeroed in on Kapelznik in the on-deck circle. "You're going to pinch-hit him, right? You can't…"

A curious silence fell over the diamond, the kind in which you can hear maybe a bumblebee or a robin and nothing else. I felt the eyes turn like a school of fish from Kapelznik to me.

"I bloody well can," I hissed right back. "Don't you dare tell me how to coach this team."

And I turned away and called to the ump for time. Because as mad as I was, I suddenly realised what I had done. I suddenly saw that fat boy standing there in the blazing sun, his round face slick with sweat as he took some hefty, cumbersome practice swings. I didn't give a damn about the game at that point. I truly didn't.

The ump granted me time and I walked gingerly up to Kapelznik, almost afraid that I'd startle him, he was that focused on his practice swings.

"Kapelznik," I began, and my voice almost broke.

He blinked his huge eyes at me, then grinned with such genuine affection that I could hardly continue.

"Bobby, look, you don't have to go up there. I can put Jesse in to pinch-hit. If you don't want to…"

My voice trailed off again, and I could hear the bodies squirming on the bleachers, I could hear every heartbeat. The lime on the first-base line stung my eyes. Very far away, I saw the skinny kid on the mound, lightly tossing the rosin bag up and down, waiting for his own big moment.

"I know, Coach," Kapelznik said, and he laid a chubby hand on my shoulder. I swear, anybody watching would have thought I was the kid and he was the man. That was just how it felt too, because something came into that boy's eyes then that I've never seen since, and maybe saw only once before, in my late father's eyes when he comforted my grandmother after my grandfather's death. How can I describe it? Not pity, not sorrow, but both of those, and something more, something that didn't seem to have anything to do with any individual person or situation but went out from there to all people in all situations, and even farther than that. It was a look that somehow took in all the heartbeats on the bleachers and in the field and the robin's chirping and my wife's tears. It was a look that said, plain as day, I know this isn't about baseball, I won't let you down.

"Play ball!" the ump shouted, and I don't even remember walking back to my spot by first base. But I was there when it all happened. I saw it. The first pitch – a called strike that made our parents groan. The second pitch – high and inside that brushed Kapelznik back and almost knocked him down. The third pitch – a change-up that he swung at and missed so early that he could have swung at it and missed again before it reached the catcher's glove. And by the time the pitcher went into his windup for the next pitch, I couldn't see Kapelznik at all for the tears and sweat running down my face; I could see only my two sons, at twelve, and know that their childhoods were over now, that I had slammed the lid down hard on that precious time. It wasn't my fault, but I had done it, just as Kapelznik wasn't my fault but I had put him at the plate.

I closed my eyes and waited for the called third strike. Maybe I was hoping that when I opened them again, my sons would be there, fully grown and ready to forgive me for what I couldn't help. Maybe I was hoping I'd open my eyes on some tropical beach somewhere where they'd never even heard of baseball. Hell, I don't know what I was thinking, except, "I'm sorry, Kapelznik, I'm really sorry."

The crack of the bat almost split me in two. I opened my eyes and saw the left and centre fielders running for the fence. There was a long silence, as of an indrawn breath. Then the yelling started. Not a cheer, not euphoric, but panicked, chaotic, awful. Because Bobby Kapelznik wasn't moving. The tying run had crossed the plate, and the winning run was almost there, but Kapelznik just stood in the batter's box, grinning. I could hear a strange, violent chorus of boys' voices and men's shouts and women's shrieks. And then one of the fathers burst around the edge of the dugout, the veins popping in his neck as he screamed, "Run! Run, you fat bastard! Run!"

That was enough for me. I bolted down the line and caught him one square on the jaw, knocking him flat. Even so, I hardly took my eyes off Kapelznik as he hitched up his pants and began to walk up the first-base line. It was beautiful. It was the most beautiful thing I'd ever seen. The grace in that stride, the pure "I'm-going-to-soak-this-up" pleasure written in every motion of the ungainly limbs. Anyone paying attention could see that this boy was going to string this moment out for the rest of his life. He was a few feet from the bag when the ball finally reached the cutoff man in short left-centre. The strange chorus intensified. For a terrible, long second, I thought they were actually going to throw him out. But I didn't yell. To my pride, I didn't even open my mouth to yell. I trusted him, you see. It was like learning how to love all over again. I just watched that big, lonely kid take a quick little skip onto the bag as the ball flew over the first baseman's head and all the boys were jumping up and down and the bloody-faced father was picking himself off the grass, and Bobby Kapelznik, teetering on that bag, turned to me and said, "See, Coach? I always walk."

Tainted Love

. . .

— I —

MOLLY QUINN, a thin, high-coloured young woman of nineteen, met the man she'd only ever know as David on the first day of her job at the neighbourhood café. Middle-aged, handsome in a rumpled, tired way, he seemed at once beleaguered and resigned, like someone still looking anxiously for something that he no longer expected to find. His voice was deep but soft, and he spoke as if he wasn't sure that anyone wanted to listen to him.

Because she was nervous, because most of the staff were older than her and prone to rapid speech peppered with sexual innuendo, Molly immediately liked this unassuming man with the watery blue eyes and the salt-and-pepper five o'clock shadow. But there was absolutely no romance in this attraction for her: he was too old. In fact, there was an almost antique quality about him. When he spoke, the sound made her think of the mahogany globe her grandfather kept on his writing desk. The sound wasn't particularly reassuring, but it had the virtue of slowing the pace. The café, especially in the late mornings and at lunch hour, was frantic with activity and noise.

The man called David smiled, said, "How are you?" and then ordered an Americano and a blueberry muffin, the same order he'd make daily for as long as Molly worked at the café, a period of eight months, until she quit to resume her university studies. She had decided to take a year off so that her student-loan debt wouldn't be quite so heavy. Though she liked reading and thought about studying literature or history, she had decided to go into nursing for practical reasons.

Over the next two months, her relationship with the man called David deepened, but in an odd way. Their exchanges were always banal but pleasant – about the weather or whatever holiday was approaching. Through comments he made, she learned that he was married and had young children – not toddlers but not teenagers either. His eyes always brightened when he spoke of his daughter, and Molly liked the brightness. It gave her a refuge from the vulgarities that swirled around in the kitchen. Guillaume, the bisexual French-Canadian prep cook, was especially graphic. He had a fondness for assessing the vegetables on his chopping board according to the size of the members of his sexual partners. And because Molly thought in terms of "members" rather than "cocks" or "dicks," because she gave off this natural reserve, Guillaume made a point of teasing her until the high colour in her cheeks blazed so red that the owner, a frenetic late middle-aged woman named Mrs. Cole, would, upon entering the kitchen, ask if she was ill.

"No, no, no," Guillaume would howl, "she is blushing, that is all. She finds my talk too – how do you say it in

English? – frank? Yes, frank. Hey Molly, maybe you should call me Frank, eh?"

But she only continued to blush and to do her job as well as she could. After the first two months, she had settled in. And that was when she noticed that the man called David, one of dozens of café regulars, mattered to her more than the others. He seemed to belong to a decorous age, in part because she noticed how he frowned whenever Guillaume emerged from the kitchen (often, the prep cook was so loud that he could be heard all over the café), but mostly because he never looked at a newspaper, never spoke of current events, and never, despite the fact that he lived nearby, ever met anyone else for coffee. He came and went like a ghost, but a material one. And unlike many other customers, he always brought his used coffee cup and muffin plate up to the counter before he left. A courteous and polite middle-aged man.

And when the change occurred, it was so subtle, at first, that Molly hardly noticed. After perhaps two weeks of it, she realised that he was always mentioning his daughter in some capacity; she had started figure-skating lessons; she was doing particularly well in math at school; she wanted a cat for her birthday. He stopped mentioning his sons. Before long, Molly understood that he was going to work his daughter into every conversation. By the fourth month, she began to feel mildly unnerved. The references were brief and innocent enough, but they were as predictable as clockwork. Normally, the staff at the café liked to dissect the habits of the regulars: the 350-pound man who ordered diet soft drinks with his three-meat breakfasts; the wild-haired businesswoman who never stopped talking on her phone; the group of new mothers whose double strollers turned the café into a congested parking lot two mornings a week. But when no one else mentioned David's constant references to his daughter, Molly assumed that he made these references only to her, or else that no one else noticed. In any case, she felt protective towards him. When he was in the café at a quiet time, and Guillaume was being his usual loud and vulgar self, she often turned the music up. It was the least she could do for the few minutes of calm he brought to her shifts.

Then the inevitable occurred, though she did not see the inevitability. David's demeanour towards her altered. He began to ask her about herself, something he had not done during the first four months. Did she like working in a café? Did she plan to keep at it? And after she mentioned university, he wanted to know about her studies, her goals for the future. It was so strange to have her future interrogated daily by someone who seemed from the past that Molly began to dread their exchanges. And once the dread began, she noticed that David's appearance had changed. Now his eyes had a brightness that seemed feverish, and his five o'clock shadow grew heavier. His plain sweaters were more rumpled, as if he'd slept in them. His voice became at once softer and more intense, like a prisoner whispering through the walls of a cell. And now he always left half of his muffin uneaten. Strangest of all, no one else seemed to notice, and she simply could not talk about it, not to her co-workers, not even to her friends and family. To do so seemed, oddly, like an act of violence.

By this time – in late winter with snow falling heavily – she had begun to think of quitting the job. And, truth be told, her decision was influenced by her decision to avoid the man called David. There was nothing frightening about him exactly – he remained as gentle a man as she'd ever met – but she felt some kind of unpleasantness approaching. It seemed connected with the heavy snow, and with her future, as if she could walk out of the café afterwards and meet the shadow of her own middle-aged self approaching through the storm and on that older arm would be a man whose eyes burned in the same disquieting way.

Molly's sleep grew disturbed. One night she woke from a dream in which Guillaume, at his cutting board, spoke ecstatically about his daughter's figure-skating lessons; the usual leer in his voice, combined with the innocent subject, was so unsettling that she could not fall back to sleep. Instead, she rose in the unfriendly silence of the grubby duplex she shared with her mother and stepfather and forced herself to study one of her biology textbooks. More than ever, the situation at work was driving her towards change and the future, and yet she could not shake the eerie feeling that it was not her own will behind the wheel. And chiding herself for being ridiculous did absolutely no good; soon, she would have to leave the café. In a few more weeks, her finances would be in sufficient shape for her to do so.

But a few days after her disturbing dream, Molly was again startled out of her plans for an uneventful change. The man called David appeared, as usual, in the late morning, but this time he was not alone. There was a child with him, a girl of perhaps eleven, whom he quickly introduced as his daughter. She could not understand why, but the appearance of this girl, this dark-haired, pretty figure-skater who wanted a cat, so unnerved Molly that she forgot to make David's Americano. He had to ask her for it after she had brought him his muffin and the hot chocolate and brownie for his daughter. Blushing as deeply as she did whenever Guillaume described a sexual act, Molly mumbled an apology and hurried into the kitchen.

"What is it, Molly?" asked the eagle-eyed Mrs. Cole. "You don't feel well? Do you need a break?"

"No, no. I'm fine. Really. I'm fine."

But she wasn't at all fine, and she knew why. She had known right away, but something in her denied the truth. The girl, David's daughter, looked like her. Remarkably so. She had the same sharp cheekbones and high colour, the same small chin and bony shoulders. The girl even moved the same way Molly did, with shy, almost apologetic gestures. Molly stared at her, and it seemed as if the large plate-glass windows beyond the girl dissolved and that she was sitting outside, in the middle of the snowfall, which descended on her like shards of glass until Molly had to close her eyes so as not to see the inevitable cuts and blood. When she opened them again, she saw that the man called David was staring at her with a curious expression on his worn, sad face, an expression that might have been concerned but which looked unmistakably like fear. But what could he possibly be afraid of? Molly busied herself bussing a few tables and resisted the urge to look in their direction. It took all the resolve she had. Finally, the bell over the entrance tinkled and, without even seeing, Molly knew that they had gone.

No one mentioned David and his daughter, even though the comings and goings of customers, especially regulars, was normally minutely dissected by the staff, including Mrs. Cole and Connie, the manager. The fact that a regular who was never seen in the café with any other person had just come in with an eleven-year-old girl should have elicited some comment. But no one spoke of it. Finally, Molly had no choice: she raised the subject herself.

Layla, a tall blonde with bright blue streaks in her hair and green eyes like an Egyptian cat, just shrugged.

"So he brought his kid in for a hot chocolate? What of it?"

Molly realised that she had to be careful. Already Guillaume had found times to tease her about David, usually when he was bored and could find nothing more interesting to do. Molly suspected that she was such an easy target that he found teasing her to be beneath him. Being careful, however, did not mean putting the incident out of her mind. After all, it was creepy the way David had stared at her. More than that, it was frightening. He had appeared to be on the verge of a scream. Molly could not understand it; she should have been screaming at *him*. No. That was silly. He'd done nothing to cause such an extreme response. In fact, he'd done very little. She took a quick inventory; he had asked her about her studies, about her plans to be a nurse. That was all. She had never felt that unpleasant sinking in her stomach that occurred whenever older men attempted to flirt with her; that happened often enough that she knew the signs well. And yet her encounters with David, though different, were now much worse. Molly knew that it had something to do with his daughter, but how could that be? The girl seemed fine; he even said she was fine. Was he lying? For what reason?

By the time she saw him again, on her next shift two days later, Molly was almost relieved by his troubled appearance; it suggested a conclusion. His eyes were bloodshot, and he clearly hadn't shaved in a while. His brown hair, which he wore long for a man his age, hung flat and dull. As he spoke, he kept picking abstractedly at a hangnail on his thumb.

"How are you, Molly? How's the studying?"

She swallowed hard. "Good. Everything's good."

He looked around the café, which was unusually quiet. Then Molly realised that it was only just after nine o'clock, at least two hours before David's normal appearance. With mounting panic, she realised that he had planned this.

"Listen," he said, and leaned his upper body toward her. But not as if to kiss her. Not that. "Have you got a minute? There's something I want to talk to you about."

The blood thudded against her ribs. She gripped the edge of the counter and looked beyond him. Outside the clear glass, the snow fell so thickly that the traffic on the road had slowed to the pace of horse-drawn wagons, their headlights like gaslight in fog. Horrified, she found she couldn't refuse him. She turned and looked over her shoulder. Why couldn't she hear Guillaume's sing-song accent or Mrs. Cole's high chatter? They were both there, she knew it. But the café was as silent as a photograph. She entered it at his side as he led the way to a corner table. The snowflakes on his hair had all melted, and he settled into a chair as if he too would melt. He rubbed his thighs, perhaps to get the blood moving in them. At the same time, the skin over his cheekbones tightened. His low voice, like an idling engine, carried the threat of noise.

"I'm guessing you just left high school. Am I right? Not too long ago. It goes fast, believe me. Thirty years."

His blue eyes smeared, though he didn't cry. His hands, on the table now, slid slowly together and apart. Molly did not think it possible, but the café grew even more silent. Where was the music? Someone had turned off the music.

"We have our reunion this spring. And there's a girl who... well, she'll be a woman now, almost fifty, like me. But people tend to stay as we remember them. It's funny..."

He leaned slightly across the table, his hands clasped, his lips trembling. Molly tensed, looked over his shoulder, hoping for another customer to walk in, or for a co-worker to appear. But the café remained empty.

"You're more like her, in my mind, than she would be now. Though you don't look like her, not at all. She was blonde and... and larger, a bigger girl."

Did his skin redden slightly? His hands trembled in their clasp. Molly's chest tightened, and she tried to make herself get up and walk away. All she had to do was say that she needed to return to work. And yet he wasn't threatening. Not really. But something that frightened her hovered around him; she found she could not meet his gaze as he continued.

"You look more like my own daughter. Maybe that's why..." A sob caught in his throat. He moaned and his hands broke apart, reconnected. "Her name was Caroline, and she was beautiful. But too quiet to be really popular. A farm girl. She went to church. I don't know, that's always made it worse, though if she really did believe in God, if she could believe, then maybe that helped her."

He no longer appeared to be talking to her. Molly looked up and saw that he spoke softly, into his chest. But even so, Molly felt herself frozen into place, apprehensive but curious now. After all, what could he do? They were in a public place with a table between them. She'd only have to scream once.

"You wouldn't know the band, of course. But they were popular in a kind of cult way and drew a pretty wild crowd.

Everyone squeezed in like sardines in front of the stage. I don't know why she was there. I was surprised. I think one of her friends must have talked her into it. It didn't seem like her kind of music. But I didn't know her. I only dreamed of her, as the other guys did. You see, it was like that. She was everything that we would have . . . a Charlie's angel. But you don't know what that is."

His words flooded out of him; he didn't seem to form them at all. Molly listened, transfixed, almost unaware of how all her muscles were clenched.

"We'd been drinking, but we weren't drunk. It would be easy enough to say that we'd had so many beers that . . . but it's a lie. At a show, beer was just too expensive, if you could even fight your way to the bar. Everything was crowded that night. And when the band finally came on, and the crowd pushed to the stage, she was right there, right in front of us."

He couldn't leave the hangnail on his thumb alone. A little spot of blood appeared on the edge of the nail, and he smudged it with his other thumb. Molly, aware that she was holding her breath, forced some air slowly through her lips and looked towards the door. As soon as a customer came in, she'd have an excuse to get away. But it was as if the world had emptied of people. A gust of snow-bearing wind rattled the plate glass window. The man called David went on in a tremulous voice.

"We were pressed in like cattle in a chute. Within minutes, people were terrified. I could see the fear on some of the faces around me, but I couldn't hear anything because the music was so loud. I knew some of the girls were screaming, though. I saw a spray of blood on a girl's face. People's heads just smashed together. It was like that at some punk concerts then. I started looking for a way out, but I could move only with the crowd. Then I saw Neal. The look on his face was different. Intense, not afraid. Like he was watching himself in a dream. His hands were around a girl in front of him. He was pressed hard against her. When she turned her head, and it was all she could turn, I..."

He choked back a heavier sob. At first, he didn't look at Molly. But when he finally did, she saw a face she'd never seen on a man before, a face without even the semblance of a mask. She saw the terrified boy in the middle-aged man. And her heart did not go out to him in pity. She was too shocked, too frightened. But she felt pity, she could taste it on her lips. The confusion held her as he went on, his voice all breaking glass.

"She was crying, her eyeliner like dark blood on her cheeks. And she screamed. Stop, she cried. It was as clear as if she'd shouted into silence. And then, even worse, Please. Please stop! But Neal's expression never changed. It was fixed, serious, linked to whatever it was his hands and the rest of his body were doing. I think I shouted at him once, and tried to move towards them. I think I did. I hope so. It was so loud and... and... not like-life... like... it was like a nightmare. And I had to get out of it."

His shoulders slumped. His hand with the bleeding thumb twitched like a dying bird on the table.

"The worst thing was, he was just like me. Ordinary. Just boys. Like a million others. And even though it wasn't me behind her, I understood. I did. I knew what was making him do what he did, I knew. I almost... I was almost jealous. Even though I hated it, hated the black tears on her face and the shout that was silent but louder than anything I'd ever heard, I was jealous. Because my hands hadn't known what his hands... because I didn't even see the possibilities. And it was that, it was *that*, as much as anything, that made me ashamed. Not what he did, but how his actions seemed to send me back years. Oh God. We were both ordinary. That's the terrible thing."

The pity had gone. Molly hadn't felt it leave her, but it wasn't there, nor did she try to recover it. All she felt now was repulsion. He was old; the boy he had been was dead before she had even been born. So why was he telling her this? Why her? Because she looked like his own daughter – was that it? Molly's mouth was dry. As the man called David gazed at her, his eyes watery, chin trembling, she wanted only to shout for help, to shout as that other girl had once shouted. But the instant the thought occurred to her, the instant she made the connection between herself and the girl at the concert who had been... yes, raped, that was the point, that was what he was crying about. In that instant, she knew herself to be violated. Her whole body began to shake.

"I didn't do anything about it," he said in a low voice. "I never said anything. Not to Neal or anyone else. We'd been friends since we were six or seven, but I could hardly even look at him after that. We stopped being friends. I wish I could say it was because I hated what he'd done, but it wasn't really that. It was because, somehow, he had left me behind. And now my daughter is growing up. She'll be around boys, ordinary boys, boys who believe that they must take that step even if it means..."

Molly pushed back from the table and her chair crashed to the floor as she stood. "Stop!" she mouthed, and hated the echo of the past even as she stood inside it. "Please. Just stop."

She saw Layla stride out from around the counter, her large hoop earrings swinging.

"What's going on? Molly, are you all right?"

"I'm sorry. I'm so . . . oh God." Heavily, the man called David picked up his gloves and grimaced as he pulled them on, as if they were barbed inside. Molly could almost see the blood spreading through his fingers. Instinctively, she stepped closer to Layla. But she did not speak; she only nodded as the man called David slouched out of the café and quickly dissolved inside the whirling snow.

Layla's sharp green eyes appraised her. "What was that all about? I thought you weren't involved with him like that."

"I'm not," Molly gasped. "He just . . . he just . . ."

Layla touched her shoulder. "It's okay, kid. Middle-aged guys are real pigs. Way worse than young guys. What did he do?"

Molly blinked rapidly. What had he done? He had told her something that had hurt him a long time ago. She still couldn't stop shaking.

Layla took charge. "You'd better have the day off. I'll tell Connie. Get your coat. I'll drive you home."

. . .

A MONTH LATER, Molly quit her job at the café and spent most of her time preparing for the start of classes in the fall. In those final weeks of work, the man called David never returned. And no one – not even Layla – commented on his absence. It was as if he had never existed, as if the snow he had walked into had borne him away. For a while, Molly thought of him, and of his daughter who looked like her.

Briefly, they dragged like a pair of anchors off the future she was slowly, carefully launching for herself. And then the chains broke, and they settled, like so much else in her life, into the capacious, accommodating past.

— II —

SHE CRIED FOR days and wouldn't go to school for over a week. Her parents were distraught. They wanted to take her to the doctor. Her father, heavy at her bedside, his wood-hard farmer's hand tentative on her shoulder, his accent even thicker than usual, begged her to tell him what the trouble was. His suffering only made hers worse. "Is it a boy?" he said, and she wondered if there was a smell coming off her, the way it came off animals. "Is that what it is? Has a boy done something?" Maybe her father, being a man, recognised some terrible change in her. Her tears came in great salt waves, each one crashing to a stillness. She only let her mother stroke her long hair, her mother who'd been a little girl hiding in tulip fields and eating the frozen bulbs to stay alive as the Germans occupied her village. Both her parents loved her deeply, she knew, since she was their only child, but they were so out-of-place here, except for with the animals and the earth. How could they even begin to understand a rock concert? They would have forbidden her to go. And what happened would just confirm for them that evil flourished the further one strayed from the farm.

She shouldn't have gone to the concert. She hadn't really wanted to. The music was just noise. But Tracy had talked her into it, as she had talked her into so many things, as she still tried to do, all these years later, saying, "You should come to the reunion. Aren't you curious to see what's happened to everybody? You didn't come to the last one." Tracy, whom she'd never told, not then or since. The telling, even to herself, was like feeling the helplessness all over again. It took a long time, and the telling finally quieted, though never permanently. Remission. That was the word. Tracy had survived breast cancer, but it could come back. Some memories were just the same, even if it was possible to live a full and enjoyable life without constantly carrying the full weight of them.

Yesterday, on the phone, the day after the reunion, Tracy had said, "You remember Dave Kerr? He was friends with Neal Sarnett, remember him? He drove that little brown Capri. I always thought he was kind of cute. His smile. Well, Dave – and nobody knows why – just up and punches Neal straight in the face. Right in the middle of the Commodore. Then he jumps on him, and two or three guys have to pull him off. He's screaming something, but nobody can hear him over the music. And the weird thing is, Neal doesn't even try to defend himself. He just lies there and takes it. And he's at least six inches taller than Dave too. Dave was short back in school and he still is. Anyway, nobody could get a word out of either one of them afterwards. Weird, isn't it? Really, Carol, you should have been there."

She is. She is when she looks up from currying Ranger's coat and sees the car turn onto the long, grassy drive and, five seconds later, hears the crunch of the gravel under his tires as Dave Kerr nears the barn. Briefly, she considers hiding. No good can come of this, at least not for her. And for him? She doesn't even want to know what his reasoning is.

By the time he opens the car door and steps into the bright sunshine, she's angry. And by the time he's moved through the barn shadow into the open doorway, his head black against the sky, she's trying to control her breathing. He has no right to be here. He has no way to punch his way back into a past they had shared briefly, and in such different ways.

She speaks softly into the horse's ear. Thirty years ago, a roan stallion named Challenger had been the one living creature who had taken her tears into his flesh without questions. That horse had carried her through, and when he died, three years later, of a twisted intestine, she had cried almost as long and as inconsolably as she had when...

Enough. Coldly, she turns and faces him.

"What do you want?"

She might have slapped him on the cheek, for he winces and turns slightly to one side. Despite the grey at his temples and the hollows under his eyes, he looks boyish, as if this meeting is taking place a year or two before they were teenagers together. For a moment, she believes that he is going to cry. His bottom lip trembles and he refuses to meet her gaze. Well, she thinks, at least he isn't going to pretend he's here for some other reason, at least he isn't going to waste time on silly comments about her appearance or the amount of time that's passed. She's thirty years older too, thirty years more tired of men and their games.

"I'm sorry," he says, his voice strangely loud in the stillness.

She's not exactly sure of his purpose, but there's no denying that he's sincere. And as the silence grows between them, as she waits for him to clarify his apology, as she watches him turn to face her and notices the broken blood vessels on his nose and the few clumps of grey grizzle around his lower lip where he'd obviously done an unsteady job of shaving, she knows only too well what his purpose is.

"Is that right?" she says between clenched teeth. "And what do you expect me to do? Give you a hug and tell you that it's all right now?"

"No. I . . . I don't . . ." He draws in a deep, rasping breath and begins to pick at a hangnail on his thumb without looking down. "I just couldn't keep getting up every morning and going through my usual day for the next thirty years without doing something. Or after that. The thought that I would die, or you would, and him, and that nothing would have changed. I had to do something."

Instinct – the instinct that comes from working with simpler, less dangerous animals than people all her life – tells her that he is genuine. But to what end? Even so, her anger subsides despite her desire to maintain it.

"Okay. You've done something. Now you can turn around and get in your car and drive away."

He takes his glasses off and wipes one of his large blue eyes with the snub of his palm. Blinking at her, he seems about five years old, and she realises that he's not likely to leave unless she takes him by the hand and leads him away. The realisation is unpleasant.

"Whatever this does for you," she says, "it's of no use to me. I'd like you to leave."

She walks past him, out of the barn and into the sunshine, as if to drag him behind her like a shadow.

"I have a daughter," he says, following, his face ghostly in the amber light. "She's eleven."

Now it's her turn to blink at him. She can smell his hangover sweat and foulness mixing with the hay and manure, and she's suddenly more disgusted than angry.

"My daughter," he starts, and his voice catches. His glasses dangle from his left hand. "There's just nothing I can do. To protect her, I mean. Nothing. I know what men are. I know what they're capable of."

He speaks as if he's not a man himself, and she wants to laugh, though nothing he says is funny. Didn't she learn the first cold lesson of what men are a long time ago, and learn it in her own skin and heart and not just the imagination?

"Well? What about it? Not all men are the same. My father loved me. My husband loves me."

"Yes! Yes!" He straightens up and lifts his glasses near his face as if they're a microscope he's about to peer into. "That's what I mean. It doesn't do any good. It doesn't matter. Love isn't any sort of protection at all. I thought, when I became a father, loving my children would be enough. But love them for what? So they can become adults, and strangers to almost everyone they'll ever meet, strangers who don't love them, who'll stand behind them at a concert and do whatever the hell they want and then just go on and have their own children and not even think about what they did?"

Panting, he puts his glasses on with shaking hands, and lowers his voice. "I saw him last night. Neal. At the reunion. In the exact same room where he did that to you. And do you know what he was doing? Texting his own daughters. Teenagers. Just like we were. Right there, on the anniversary of what he did to you, in almost the exact same spot, he was texting his daughters and smiling that fucking smile.

I would have killed him if they hadn't pulled me off. It was just as if he'd . . . as if he'd . . ."

She knows what he means, that it was as if Neal Sarnett had raped his daughter. And though she's both appalled and not at all surprised by the magnitude of his ego, she can't quite bring herself to hate him for loving his child so much, even if what he seems to have wakened to is a world women have to wake to so much earlier, and with much more immediate consequences. Despite herself, or because of herself, she makes a small offering.

"There's nothing you can do about other men." She locks eyes with him. "What happened hurt me. It was as if I hardly knew the world at all. And it took me a long time to trust anyone. But it didn't destroy me."

"But it could have. It could have been worse. Some other time, you could have been killed."

Sighing, she looks beyond his drawn face to the tops of the poplar windbreak where a few crows have just landed. Hasn't she felt this same fear all over again – doesn't she feel it whenever she can't stop herself – her two daughters away at university, negotiating the old channels between the sexes? Hasn't she worried every day of their sweet lives that she would somehow transfer some of that terrible fear to them? She's worked too hard for too long to let some guy's self-pity bring that darkness back upon her. She wants to say to him, your fear can take the joy of life away from your daughter too, your fear can stand behind her all her life and take and take. It isn't the same, but you don't have the right to make her afraid. She wants to say, why is it always about the men, why are you even here, you're not here for me at all, or for your daughter, you're here only for yourself, and you want to take something that hasn't been given. I didn't ask you to come, why should I be responsible for making your memories easier for you? She wants him to understand the selfish violence that often masquerades as love and forgiveness for men, but the vastness of the whole subject just exhausts her, as if she's waking up again, the morning after the concert, beginning the long work of breaking that mountain into a boulder into a single stone. But never powder, never so small, always something painful to swallow.

"Have you ever ridden a horse?" she asks, surprising herself.

He blinks even more rapidly, his eyes like tiny captive birds behind his glasses. "No. No, I never have."

Relieved to be moving and acting, she strides to the barn, saddles Ranger, and leads him into the sunshine.

"That's a big animal," he says, and laughs nervously.

"Stallions are big, yes. And powerful." She pats the horse on his cord-like neck. He snorts and lifts his head back, showing his enormous teeth. The waft of his musk rises to meet the sun's heat. The horse slaps his tail at a blowfly.

"Come on. Up you get." She nods to direct him to the proper side for mounting. "I'll help you."

He hesitates, and she knows, in an instant, that he doesn't trust her, that his fear extends beyond imaginary evils. And the knowledge is dangerous; she feels it enter her bloodstream like an elixir, a strange power. She can do anything with it, and he's helpless to stop her. His fear, and the smell of the horse and the hot earth, make her heart pound.

In a moment, he has swung himself awkwardly into the saddle and balanced there like an empty hand puppet. His two hands are white on the horn. When she holds out the reins to him, he just stares, open-mouthed, and his helplessness infuriates her. Now Ranger shifts his rippling bulk. If she makes even the slightest motion of command, the horse will gallop into the field and this man and his self-pity and helplessness will be flung into the air and broken on the hard ground. For a few seconds she feels the power coursing through her veins, the same power coursing through the horse, coursing through the old channels all daughters have to cross, men watching coldly from the banks, and she only has to open her mouth and drop the reins and stand back and watch the blood and the sun mingle in the dust. It is so tempting and easy, this power, so thrilling, and she feels herself succumbing to it. The world blurs in her vision. She sees without seeing. The reins in her palms connect to nothing. She only has to let go. The sky, the sun, the barn, the years, her parents' graves: the whole dark force of living breathes on her neck. It would take so very little to let go. The horse adjusts. The earth with it.

When she finally opens her eyes to the moment, he seems so small in the saddle, as if she's seeing a man on a horse from three fields away. Once, after her second daughter was born, she terrified herself by looking at the baby this same way, objectively, almost coldly, trying to remember what the nature of her relationship to this new life was. But she isn't terrified now, only strangely unmoved. Here's a man who'd once been a boy trembling beside her in biology class as they completed some lab assignment together. And if he isn't quite so unaware of his power now, he's still a boy with a boy's awkward, inconvenient ego.

The reins are slick with sweat. The horse's motion is the earth's too. She ought to let go, let the man feel in his body what he feels only in his mind, let him understand the indifferent power as his daughter will have to understand it, or at least deflect it.

But somehow, as the concert of stillness and pulse and light crashes around her, it is her own life, her own body, that she holds, her tears cried out on the mane, and more love than hate on the open sunlit field before her as she leads the horse and silent rider gently on.

Bartleby, the Sessional

. . .

WHEN THE university he'd been poorly employed at for the past twelve years decided to eliminate three-year sessional teaching contracts, Jerris Johns started sleeping in the clothes he taught in. This behaviour was both practical and psychological; practical because his landlord would never heat the complex sufficiently at night, and psychological because the institution's further attack on the Humanities made him feel as naked as Lear on the heath. Where he could once make a desperate three-year plan of survival, he now would have to make an even more desperate plan every twelve months.

In the most recent department meeting with the Dean of Arts, Jerris had screwed his courage to the sticking place to protest the decision. The dean, a slick-haired fast-talker whose favourite strategy was to lower his voice and say, "Listen, I taught in the English department for years. I'm one of you, I get where you're coming from," nodded understandingly and then, grinning like Uriah Heep, discussed the drop in oil prices and therefore provincial post-secondary funding. When Jerris looked around in exasperation for support, he saw that the tenured faculty – which had dwindled to fifty percent of the department now – mostly stared at their phones, while the other sessionals appeared, like inmates on death row, to be waiting for a pardon that they knew would never come.

That was early September. It was now mid-October and snowing and sub-freezing already. Too bad for the trick-or-treaters, Jerris thought, though few children went door-to-door on Halloween night anymore. Even the little kids had had the joy sucked out of their lives. Jerris had already stopped counting the number of students he taught who consumed opioids and antidepressants like Skittles to combat what they felt but mostly couldn't recognise or accept as a kind of mirthless servitude. Increasingly, he saw his students as motionless structures of exposed nerve-endings, and himself as a robotic fount of useless knowledge. His area of scholarly research – the first books that famous American writers published after their masterpieces (Herman Melville's *Pierre, or the Ambiguities*; Joseph Heller's *Something Happened*; etc) – had never gained traction, and his efforts to secure a tenure-track position, even in such unhallowed places as Idaho and South Dakota (or was it North? He couldn't remember), had become reflex actions rather than affairs of hope.

Even so, Jerris Johns, approaching forty, was a conscientious and effective teacher. Or at least he always had been. There'd never been any reason for the department to question either his pedagogy or his behaviour. Ordinary looking with a gentle manner, he was popular with students but not too popular. Over the years, sensing that the generations below him would have an even harder time economically than he'd had, he started lowering his grading standards, and that move ensured that his classes of introductory rhetoric and analysis always filled up (every student, regardless of degree program, had to complete six English credits). The more enthusiastic and talented of his students now made him feel both despondent and guilty. He was no longer young enough to sell them illusions.

Jerris woke this particular October day an hour before his alarm went off, and lay on his back, watching the huge Rorschach blot of the blue spruce outside his bedroom window shift around in the wind. As he pondered the fluid black motion, the stress in his body began to rise. By the time the alarm sounded, he had already reached for his laptop and pulled the duvet over his head. The screen's underwater light was painful, but he felt a great relief as he posted a notice to his students that class was cancelled. Technically, he was supposed to alert the department of his decision, but he just didn't feel obliged at the moment to follow the rules. Besides, what were they going to do? Threaten him with precarious employment? Smiling, but without pleasure, he rolled over in his sweater and jeans and fell asleep.

Three hours later, standing in front of his day's second class (he had been given only two courses for each term), Jerris noticed that the attendance was very low, about thirty percent. Perhaps the inclement weather had kept the students home. Jerris couldn't blame them. Rotely, he returned to the matter of identifying thesis statements.

The next morning, with the snow heavier and the thermometer dropping, Jerris cancelled another class, again without alerting the department. This time, he couldn't rally as the day progressed and, his heart racing a little, he nixed his afternoon class too. That evening, when not a single student had emailed him, he realised that the cancellations were probably a relief to them, overworked and underslept as most of them were. By the end of the week, when he also realised that the students weren't contacting the department either, he slowly began to formulate a breathtaking plan to counter the desperate financial planning he'd have to do at year's end. At first, he laughed at the idea, all the values of his Protestant-though-secular work ethic immediately going into a kind of immune system overdrive. But as Sunday evening arrived, and with it the unconquerable desire not to prepare for teaching, Jerris felt almost giddy. Why go to campus at all? The inevitable future of lecturing would be virtual anyway, if not actually done by artificial intelligence, so why not get a head start and even go one step further by not lecturing, period? Of course, he couldn't just vanish entirely; he'd have to maintain some connection with his students, perhaps show up every third class or so. The rest of the time, he could send out twice-daily emails, creating the semblance of responsibility. As for assignments, well, what student would complain if he simply reduced the number of required essays from three to two? Or even from three to one? Under his warm duvet, chuckling as he tapped the keyboard, Jerris felt younger and more exultant than he had since he was a teenager whose love of literature had nothing to do with the draining forces of getting and spending.

By the third week, he knew he was in the clear. And because he wasn't depressed, he began to go out – to art galleries, bookstores, the library, even to matinees. In fact, he could hardly wait to go to bed each night so that he could get up and live the next day. He didn't even care that the weather had grown even colder, almost minus fifty with wind chill. Indeed, the temperature was his best ally, for each cancelled class had a greater chance of coming as a relief to his students. The stillness and fragility of the air – the sheer uniqueness of such severe cold – only heightened his feeling that he'd escaped from a sick world into a healthy one. Hadn't Mann's main character in *Death in Venice* died from making the reverse journey? Jerris couldn't remember, so he added *Death in Venice* to the growing pile of pleasure reading beside his bed.

When students finally emailed their first assignments, Jerris glanced at them and gave each one a mark at least two grades higher than deserved. Not surprisingly, when he sent the grades out, no one complained or requested a meeting. Jerris calculated that his hourly wage had now shot up from about forty dollars to three hundred dollars. Feeling rich, and almost successful, he bought some new clothes and started making dates with women on Tinder and other dating sites. The subsequent sexual liaisons only confirmed his sense of regeneration; he took to his new life as naturally as a gander takes to migration.

Then the email arrived. It was from a student in his morning course, a young man whose name didn't conjure up any image in Jerris's mind. Had the student even attended class? Well, at least the note was respectful and composed in complete sentences. Dear Professor, it began, I am a student in your English 103 course and I would like to meet with you to discuss my essay. Also, I would like to ask your opinion about doing a degree in English. What would be a convenient time for me to come to your office?

Jerris's initial reaction was irritation. Things had been coasting along so nicely that he believed he wouldn't have to talk with any students or colleagues – and hardly even see them either – right to the end of the term. As it was, he could barely remember what office he'd been assigned (it changed each semester, and he generally shared it with two other sessionals). Meeting a student was inconvenient enough; maybe he could ask the young man to meet at a café off campus in his neighbourhood. But even then, the request was a nuisance. Once his irritation wore off, however, Jerris read the email again and a feeling of pity nagged at his heart. A degree in English? Now? In a world run entirely by and for STEM, a world in which the Humanities themselves were Inhumane for the illusions they continued to market to impressionable and idealistic youth?

Reluctantly, Jerris replied to the email, suggesting that the young man meet him at a Starbucks just down the block from Jerris's apartment. Then he realised that he'd probably have to show up to the next morning's class, since clearly he now had at least one student who wasn't just taking the course for the required credit.

Of course, the weather had to be just as cold as it had been of late, with the streets empty and the hoar frost cracking on the elms all along the avenue as Jerris walked to the bus stop. Looking down an alley, he saw a mangy coyote sniffing around a garbage can, and the image of desperate privation reminded him of his failing and doomed academic career. Depressed for the first time in over a month, Jerris had to build up his courage just to walk into the classroom.

To his surprise, no one was there. Not a single youth sat behind a laptop gazing at flickering images. Not even the young man who'd sent the email. Well, Jerris decided, it was miserable weather, and he had cancelled two weeks of classes already. Even so, the emptiness of the room was breathtaking – and a little frightening. How quickly the students had adjusted to Jerris's new schedule. But surely someone interested in taking an English degree would make an effort to attend class, at least immediately after sending such an email. Then again, Jerris knew only too well that the behaviour of students was rarely anything if not perplexing. Maybe this young man, whatever his name was, intended only to meet with Jerris privately once and then revert to form. Maybe he had a certain scorn for his contemporaries – Jerris remembered having such an attitude himself in his undergraduate years – that made attending class almost embarrassing.

Well, it didn't matter. Jerris stood stiffly behind the lectern for five more minutes, staring with dread at the open doorway, half-expecting all the students to burst inside in one mad rush, filling every corner, pressing hard against him until he couldn't breathe or escape, dozens of students, hundreds, thousands, all shouting questions at him about thesis statements, all demanding to know where he'd been for the past month. Finally, after wiping the sweat off his forehead with a trembling hand, he left the classroom.

Walking rapidly along the hallway, he passed a young male student, an ordinary looking kid wearing a ball cap and a punk T-shirt (The Clash, was it? The Ramones?) who hesitated, his eyes locked on Jerris's own, before he grinned as if with pain and continued on. Jerris looked back over his shoulder. Could that have been the emailer? He had a sudden intuition that it was, but before he could decide what to do, the student rounded a corner and disappeared. Jerris wasn't even sure he'd be able to recognise him in the Starbucks the next day.

That night, feeling ill, he cancelled a Tinder rendezvous and spent several hours playing a video game he'd loved a decade ago. The bright lights and rapid motion, which sometimes made him feel seasick, actually had the opposite effect. Grounded and relaxed, he decided to check his university email before going to bed. The only note in his inbox immediately alarmed him.

> Dear Professor,
>
> I'm sorry. I won't be able to make the meeting tomorrow. I suffer from anxiety and I'm having a bad time just now. Can we reschedule for next week?

To his amazement, Jerris didn't feel relieved. On the contrary, the idea of going through an entire week before meeting the student made him anxious. He had half a mind to reply with a firm no, saying that his time was valuable and that he had other matters to attend to. Instead, without any sensation in his fingertips, he sent a note suggesting the same time and place next week and added that he hoped that the student would be feeling better soon.

The temperatures warmed enough during the week for several snowstorms to cover the city. Venturing out only to get coffee, Jerris felt that the snow had muted something inside him too. He skittered through the streets like a piece of foolscap. Twice, early in the morning before the sun was up, he saw the same mangy coyote under a streetlamp; the animal seemed to stare at him, but with haughty indifference. The other half of Jerris's mind wanted to throw a snowball at the creature. But the coyote's stillness and mockery, so human and familiar, held him back.

By the day of the meeting with the student, Jerris was weak from lack of food. Cooking – or going out to eat – involved too much effort. In the morning, he tried to preoccupy himself by calling up some of his unpublished articles on the computer. Had he really written them? Delivered them at conferences? He couldn't imagine the person who had done such work. Wrenching himself away from the lean, haggard reflection in the computer screen, he plunged into the storm. The ongoing snowfall seemed to fall over all accomplishment, obliterating his past and obscuring his future. Almost staggering, his own breath like toxic clouds, Jerris made it to the Starbucks.

Not surprisingly, the café was almost empty. Two middle-aged women sat talking at a small table in a corner, a giant bald man in a pumpkin-orange sweater grinned foolishly into a laptop at another corner table, while a magenta-haired barista waited at the till to take the next order. Only when he had stepped further inside did Jerris see the shrunken, scarved figure in a black toque slumped at a table against the far wall. Annoyed by the increase in his heart rate, Jerris approached the figure and, clearing his throat, said, "Hi. You must be . . ."

A violent bout of coughing smothered his words. The student, looking up through watery eyes, the scarf wrapped in python folds around the lower half of his face, apologised faintly.

"It's good of you to come, Professor. This day's not . . . not exactly . . . I mean, I wouldn't have blamed you if you didn't show up."

Jerris nodded, and then, almost deafened by the throbbing in his temples, asked the student if he could get him anything.

"No, no thank you. I mean, there isn't anything that . . . nothing you can buy at a Starbucks." The watery eyes rippled. "I got a tea already." He moved one mittened hand out from the thick fold of his worn parka, revealing the familiar cup with the mermaid logo.

After ordering his coffee and waiting at the counter to receive it, Jerris joined the student at the table. For a painful moment, neither of them spoke, just mechanically lifted their cups to their lips as some dead crooner – Sinatra or Tony Bennett – smoothly filled the heated air.

"I just read *Moby-Dick*," the student suddenly started, his voice so raspy and weak that Jerris had to lean towards him to catch the words. "You know the character Pip? The boy who jumps out of the whale boat and gets left behind for a whole day? Just floating in the ocean, thinking, not knowing if anyone is going to come back for him." The student tightened the scarf at his throat. "That's just how I feel. Like Pip. Before he goes mad, I mean. Or as he's going mad maybe. Floating there. Just floating. Except heavy too. Kind of like a statue of a person. If it could float." He coughed so that the whole oversized parka shook. Recovering, he said, "But I guess I'm supposed to think about Ahab. Or the whale. Not some lost boy. I mean, it's not exactly *Peter Pan*."

Did he smile beneath the scarf? Was there mocking laughter in his words? Jerris couldn't tell. The student's voice was so weak, barely audible enough to possess a tone. Besides, the café was so hot that Jerris found himself sweating heavily, even though he'd removed his thick coat and the first layer beneath it. The student, however, not only kept all his winter protection on, but he also looked frozen, as if he truly was treading water in the middle of an ocean at night. His forehead, unfurrowed, gleamed like polished marble.

At a loss for an appropriate response, Jerris merely repeated, "No, it's not *Peter Pan*." Then, in the painful echoing silence that followed, he tried to rally. "But J.M. Barrie must have read Melville. I mean, the crocodile that pursues Captain Hook. That's really just the whale and Ahab, isn't it? Except Hook tries to get away from the crocodile, of course. He doesn't go looking for it."

Jerris's voice trailed off. Why did his words seem so completely pointless? The student didn't want to talk about *Peter Pan*. He obviously didn't even want to talk about Melville or Pip either. So, what *did* he want to talk about?

Jerris took a sip of coffee and let the silence close around them both. Even the grinding of the espresso machine sounded miles distant. The student, meanwhile, held his tea-filled cup like a small, wounded animal inside his parka. He didn't bother to lift his head when he spoke again.

"The truth is... I think I'm dying. And when I read, everything I read tells me that I might as well."

"What?" Jerris looked around wildly, but neither the conversing women, the giant bald man, or the barista noticed that he'd almost shouted. "What do you mean you're dying? What's wrong with you? Have you been to a doctor? You... you..."

"I don't have any energy. I could hardly make it here. And wherever I go, I'm just so heavy. But I float. Like Pip. It's only a matter of time."

"Time?" Jerris had to put his cup down because his hands trembled so much. "What do you mean?"

"Before I sink. Or before they find me and I've already gone mad."

"Before who finds you? What are you talking about? You're not in the ocean."

The student lifted his head as if by an invisible winch. His eyes, which really did look full of seawater, floated in his marble skin. "You know? They. The ones who leave you all alone. Who don't know. So that you have to become one of them to survive."

Jerris clutched his hands together to stop them from shaking. Hot and sweating, he removed another shirt until he was down to just one thin layer. When he had pulled his head through the shirt's small opening, and looked across the table, the student seemed to have drifted away by several feet. Jerris heard the raucous shrieking of gulls out of the café speakers. His temples throbbed like surf pounding the shore. Salt spray stung his eyes. The student's scarf unwound, and his mouth opened in a tiny O. Jerris's arms swung like oars as the student's chair drifted farther away, his upper body slumped on the table, the cup sliding from his grip and blood spilling out of it across the intervening air. By the time Jerris had struggled to his feet, the student was crying inside the gull-cry, pleading for help. When Jerris ran forward, when he grabbed the student around his midsection, a searing pain flashed across his own ribcage as the flesh of the young man dissolved and Jerris found himself sinking under the lights and the sounds and the unending snow until he was heavy and floating and the crying of his voice couldn't make consciousness turn back to recover him.

Several minutes later, after he had been helped to his feet by the giant bald man, after he had told the two middle-aged women that he didn't need an ambulance, after he had gratefully accepted a new espresso from the barista and assured everyone that he was fine, that he sometimes suffered from dizzy spells and that the cold, fresh air would perk him right up, Jerris slowly made his way home and crawled, fully clothed, into bed. Shivering, unable to stop his teeth from chattering, he lay in the foetal position and tried to quiet the shrieking of the gulls and the desperate crying of the student as the near bedroom wall widened into a blank, inanimate horizon. At long last, he either passed out or fell asleep.

When he came to, he still had almost no warmth in his body, and remained in bed as the last threads of twilight turned into a solid block of dark that destroyed the terrible white sky of the room. But slowly the nightmare passed, the student's scarved face with the submarine eyes faded, and Jerris didn't even worry about why the young man had left in such a hurry – after all, Jerris realised that he wasn't being paid enough to do social and psychiatric work in addition to correcting comma splices.

In fact, the Starbucks encounter, unsettling as it had been, finally freed Jerris to make a last bold move. He emailed both of his classes, told the students to email him their second assignments (which would be their last), and then didn't even bother to cancel the remaining three weeks of the term. He just didn't show up, nor did he check his email again until he knew that the students' assignments would be in his inbox. Indulging himself by ordering through Skip the Dishes every night, by deleting all his academic writing, and by donating several boxes of scholarly journals, textbooks, and reference works to Goodwill, Jerris understood that his floating idyll was both reckless and doomed, that the world like a blood-filled whale boat would eventually return for him, just as the pathetic student had said it would.

And yet, when he finally decided to submit his final grades (after randomly assigning generous marks) and saw the email from the chair of the department requesting a meeting in her office, he was both saddened and anxious. At first, he considered quitting, and then letting the consequences of that decision play out, even to the point of suicide, for he understood that his life had come right to that edge where the horizon would always be a lifeless sliding wall. But then he decided not to give the institution an easy way out. Let them do their own dirty work, he thought. Let them use the axe for once instead of the thousand little knife nicks.

The chair smiled as she gestured for him to sit. She brought out a sheaf of papers from her desk. Her smile widened as she complimented Jerris on his term – the student evaluations were over-the-top positive, and the department had received dozens of requests from students wanting to enrol in his classes for next term. The dean, she said, wanted to reward him. Though it was no longer institutional policy, he recognised the value of Jerris's pedagogy and wanted to offer him a full-time three-year contract at a higher wage. In addition, the chair went on, the department would like to honour him with a certificate of undergraduate teaching excellence.

Jerris smiled back. The walls of the office receded. He signed the contract, shook the chair's hand, and walked out like a pardoned man into the crowded arterial pathways of the young.

Five years later, he was earning a six-figure salary in administration and building a fine collection of vintage jazz on vinyl.

As Green as the Grass Grows

. . .

MY SISTER WAS telling me about her earliest memories, and I was listening as intently as almost fifty years before, when we were children together in a town of such lush beauty and abundant life that we might have been living inside one of the thick books of fairy tales she read aloud from, a book as heavy and dripping with magic as the great salmon our father carried home from the river, his index finger hooked under the gills, a trail of blood spots dripping off the geisha-fan fishtails like Hansel and Gretel's trail of breadcrumbs, except it was tomcats creeping out of the tall grass of the vacant lots and not feeding birds that erased the trails and left us in the middle of this forest without our parents and no possible way to return to a world that was no longer there.

"I'm standing at the top of the stairs above the plumbing shop," she said, "and I can see them bringing her in. Grandpa has his arm around her shoulders and she's crying in a way I've never seen anyone cry before and maybe haven't since, crying – I don't know – as if she was trying to dissolve her bones. I thought that if they let her keep crying, she was going to disappear, with maybe just her eyes and her mouth left, like the Cheshire cat. I'd been reading *Alice*, I remember. Or maybe, you know how it is, I saw her like that at the foot of the stairs, and a year later I read *Alice*, and now the two memories have become the same memory."

My sister was fifty-seven, and the long black hair of my first storyteller had turned grey and there were no rainbow-coloured ribbons in it or bangles and the freckles on her pale skin had long since burned off. I was fifty-two, grey-grizzled, but my eyes still looked for magic in voices and words. Between us, as always, stood the stillborn child whose sex we never learned, now fifty-four, a character not quite from a story unless a story is the same as life. My sister held our sibling's one hand, and I held the other, because in school we had made the paper cut-out rows of figures and could not bring ourselves to use the scissors that Time kept thrusting towards us.

"Where was Grandma?" I said. "Where was Dad?" And already I was a boy again, asking question after question. "Where was love? Where was forgiveness?"

"Grandma was there." My sister's voice turned icy. She looked beyond me, seemed to subdue a shudder. At first, I thought she was joking, was merely imitating the mock-horror tone she long ago teased me with whenever I asked where our mother was: "She's not coming back. She's lo-o-o-st in the dis-t-a-a-nce." My sister stayed that way for half a minute, and then blinked and shook her head. "At least I imagine she was there. Somehow, I can hear her laughing more than I can see her. Maybe that makes it worse. If I could see her face, then the laughing wouldn't seem to belong to . . ." She paused, gazing even more intently at the same spot over my head.

"To who?"

My sister visibly shuddered this time. "Not who. What."

I might have laughed if not for her uncharacteristic stillness, which had lasted long beyond the limits of a joke. A criminal lawyer with a busy practice, she couldn't afford to waste too much time on humour. In fact, I was surprised that she seemed so willing to delve into the past, even if she sometimes did so as a kind of clinical exercise in arranging evidence.

"Haven't you ever thought it was odd," she said, "that no one ever knew the sex of the baby Mom lost?"

I blinked vacantly, and she added, "It was basically full term, after all."

"How do you know that?"

My sister lowered her eyes, but they did not return to normal seeing. "Dad let it slip one time." She spoke the next sentence and, horrified, I saw her sitting at the top of a long staircase, in a patterned skirt with matching socks and hair ribbons, gazing down at me. "I've always thought it was a girl. I've always known I had a sister. But . . ."

I wanted to break the tension somehow, but I seemed intuitively to realise that I was the spellbound listener again, even if there was no open book.

". . . not a human sister."

She turned her head to the front door and gazed so intently that I expected the door to open at any second. The little girl and the long staircase, which had seemed so real, had vanished. But my sister's face wore a child's look of rapt curiosity that bordered on terror.

"What did you mean about Grandma's laughter?" I tried to say. "Who else could it belong to?"

The silence deepened around us. I felt a draught and knew that the door had opened and closed without moving.

"Him too?" my sister asked of the air in the room. And then to me, "Come on."

. . .

WE STEPPED INTO the old neighbourhood, and I knew at once that all our dead were alive, even those who were dead before we were born. It was a Saturday night, late, in summer. I could smell the rich musk of salmon wafting over the dyke and, from the opposite direction, curiously, the equally heavy smell of buttered popcorn. The vacant lots across from our house all had cars parked in their cracked driveways – and the three houses that had been vacant all my childhood had curtains in their windows. The grass, too, which had always been waist-high in summer, was cut to a couple of inches, and the fruit orchards had obviously been pruned. But the same grey gravel road lay between the properties and led towards the main street on the opposite side of the lots.

As my sister and I walked along it, the streetlights suddenly pinged on – two of them, at the same time, like giant sunflowers in time-lapse photography. I looked to the dyke road and saw the fuzzy lights at each corner and felt that we had entered some arena illuminated, like a bull ring, for violence. Except all I could hear was the melodic whistling of a red-winged blackbird. A moment later, I saw the plumbing shop and the second-floor apartment just to our left, but we turned the opposite way – the three of us, for I knew we were not alone here – and came to a small building with CINEMA in neon red letters buzzing above a double-sided doorway and a glassed-in ticket booth. To one side of the door, also under glass, hung a movie poster with a lioness and cubs pictured on it. But no one sat in the booth, and no one stopped us as we opened the heavy door and walked out of the buttery dusk into the buttery dark.

Immediately, I heard the whirring of the projector and saw its beam. As my eyes adjusted to the change in light, I saw that the theatre was empty, that the bottom halves of the hinged velvet seats stood straight up as tombstones, and that, on the screen, the beam of light revealed two old women who looked enough alike to be sisters, though one was thin and bony with a pinched face and the other was moon-faced with full lips inexpertly smeared with red lipstick.

"You're old and you have nothing," the thin woman hissed. "All your acting won't help you now." And she slapped the other woman's helpless, blinking face. But when the crying started, it came from a seat down near the front, a terrible sobbing, like the gulping of frogs at twilight.

"We never wanted to hurt you," the helpless woman on the screen said in a frantic voice. "He . . . he . . . was . . ."

"Liar!" The thin old woman slapped the other woman even harder. "You wanted anything in pants. And now you're paying for it. Now where will you go? Now who will have you?"

I watched our grandmother's unpleasant smile fall apart into a mocking laughter as she hit her sister yet again. Then the theatre door opened behind us, and our grandfather, the plumber, came in and gently approached our great-aunt and lifted her up and placed his arm around her shoulders and said, "It's all right now, I'll take you home, it's all right."

They stood at the foot of the long staircase in the beam of the projector's light and my sister gazed down at them while a piercing laughter circled and settled like a flock of feeding gulls. Then our grandmother dove at our grandfather and struck at him with her tiny hands at the ends of her bony arms while our great-aunt slumped to the hard floor and wept her fat, ungirdled body into a widening pool of blood.

"She had a miscarriage," my sister said, halfway between a question and a statement, halfway between a gasp and a sob.

Then the screen went blank, the beam disappeared, and a dusty sunlight caught my sister's face and turned it towards me.

"It was a girl. She would have been our aunt."

"How do you know?" But I could tell my sister was listening to a current of sound I couldn't hear. After a moment, I felt two pairs of eyes studying me.

My sister spoke, but not to me. "She's forty-four." The realisation that she meant my wife sent a shudder from my scalp to the base of my spine. "There'd be risk," my sister went on. "She's never had a child. It would be very hard."

"But we talked it all over years ago," I said in a whisper. "We decided years ago."

The theatre collapsed without sound around us, collapsed like shadows. We stood in the ruins, staring back towards our childhood.

"I remember when they tore it down," my sister said. "Do you?"

Because I wasn't sure that she spoke to me, I didn't respond out loud. But I did remember. I remembered the last film, the only one I ever saw there: *Born Free.* It was about a lioness raised from a cub by humans. I could see the tawny grass of the African savannah, a jeep moving through it – but nothing else.

"You could smell butter on the air all summer." My sister lifted her head, and I had a horrifying vision of grass blades pushing through a grave. "You couldn't even smell the salmon, their blood. Don't you remember? Dad went over and got a couple of the theatre seats. Red as sockeye flesh, but softer. He soldered one chair to the deck of his boat. You must remember? There was always a faint scent of butter on the boat."

She sighed, longer than the summer's reach. "He wanted to put the other one by his father's grave, but they wouldn't let him."

My voice caught, then carried over the generations. "Why not? And how do you . . ."

"For her sake. Oh, if I'd only been a few years older, I'd have understood everything so much better. Our grandfather loved her, don't you see? And Grandma knew it and tormented them both. I always knew she was vicious. I just sensed it, and then, of course, I *did* see things, they're here." She touched both temples lovingly, as if her skull was a vase.

"So he burned it instead. In the backyard. The only time I ever saw him cry. Charred as black as the salmon's eyes or the spaces between the stars."

My sister was crying now, holding herself perfectly still. "He didn't know what terrible price he'd have to pay. All those years, sitting on that theatre seat and looking out over the river and missing his father, half-convinced that his mother wasn't who he'd always thought she was."

"The theatre seats?" My lips were dry.

"Because she'd been a performer. A piano player. For the silent movies. And they could meet there, in the dark, even if they didn't sit exactly side-by-side." My sister looked down from the top of a staircase, and I wondered if that would be the only look she'd ever give the world from now on. "It was hell for them both. And he'd already been through hell. That was why he turned to her. Turning to his wife... you don't remember Grandma, do you? Compassion wasn't in her nature. She tired of his nightmares very quickly, wanted him to get on with things." My sister nodded, as if someone was silently passing her information. "She would call me the devil's child and mean it. Once – I couldn't have been more than four – she called me a little bitch."

"Wait. Just wait." I fought with mounting desperation to orient myself to the quotidian world. These relatives were all dead decades before, in a previous century, and my sister and I were responsible middle-aged adults. Perhaps, because we'd been raised in the midst of great natural beauty at a time when children were often left alone with only their own imaginations for company, we were more susceptible to the undreamt-of energies of existence. Or perhaps we were simply prey to the phantasms of growing old. It was impossible to tell, since we had never grown old before. I took a deep breath, closed my eyes, and tried to marshal the disturbing facts.

Our grandmother had been a nasty woman, impatient with her husband's trauma after the trenches. Our grandfather had turned to our great-aunt for comfort. There had been a pregnancy, but no child. Our father might or might not be our grandmother's son. But who was speaking to my sister? And what did my wife have to do with any of this?

An icy hand closed around mine. My eyes flashed open. But my sister stood several feet away, gazing into the late summer sunlight sifting down onto the old neighbourhood.

She said, "The dead can trouble the unborn too. Our grandmother's evil reached beyond this world." My sister turned to me, her face half shadow, half light. "Dad always loved his auntie. She was so kind to him, so loving. And Grandma was dead by then too, you understand. Dad figured there could be no harm."

"What harm? What do you mean?" I couldn't tell if the cold air on my face was just the twilight or someone's breath.

"If the baby was going to be a girl," my sister explained, "Mom and Dad had decided to name her after his aunt."

"Who might have been his mother. Yes, I understand."

My sister said coldly, "No, you don't," and started to walk back the way we had come. When I was abreast of her again, the coldness now all over my body, she spoke as if the planet was sinking under, rather than sailing through, space.

"Our sister was killed in the womb for spite."

I grabbed her shoulder. The lawyer's rational expression stared unblinkingly back.

"Given what humans are," she said, "why wouldn't there be murder on the other side? Why wouldn't all the pain and hatred carry across?" Her expression softened. "And justice too. Our sister wants to be here. She wants to be human."

I stared across the waving lots of bluejoint grass towards the harbour where a hundred masts of the fishing fleet stood higher than church steeples. Some swallows dipped below the phone lines, chasing termites. The sunlight lay heavy as egg yolk on the black-limbed cherry and apple trees. I could see our father sitting in the theatre seat on the deck of his boat and crying. But only in my mind. Everything else was material – the people were shades. The dead people. Only the living could feel the heavy sunlight, pick and taste an apple.

Then I understood my wife's part in the drama. And my own role clarified into a fragile tangibility, as a sperm and egg clarify into something just as fragile and real. The coldness did not leave my body – this was no fairy tale, and the magic was only the magic that surrounds our ignorance.

"Blood tests," my sister said. "And they used to check for insanity in the family. For what could be passed on. Genetics." She took my other hand – my free hand – in hers, and the paperchain was almost complete. "They ought to check for humanity. If you had humans in your ancestry, that's going to be passed on. No clean start." Softly, she spoke my wife's name. "Not even Martha knows what she will carry on of her own blood. I don't mean cells. Look at our family. I mean a boy with the brains of his best friend splattered over his face, I mean a man who had to drink so that he could climb down into a basement to check someone's pipes, I mean a woman who couldn't love and a woman who could only love. Our sister needs a way to get here."

I nodded, but something steeled in me, cold as the touch of death. A child, who would be, in fact, a sibling. And a reparation of almost-ancient wrongs. But it seemed like another crime rather than justice.

"And what will that child carry?" I said.

"What we all carry." My sister tightened her grip on my hand, and something did the same to my other hand. "The damage, the hurt. But the promise too. Just like us. What happened in the trenches, and how he fought to survive it all those years. A hundred other things. Even the hurt our grandmother carried. Of course..." I felt her shudder pass through me. "Sometimes evil is just evil."

What was my life, I thought. Neither happy nor unhappy, turned to the past, turned to the future, buffeted by a violent world I had no control over. Yet some force sustained my life – call it blood, call it memory, call it the soft paws of a summer sun walking in consort, if only briefly, with a human will. I heard a voice whisper, "Please," and it might have been my great-aunt's voice, my father's, my missing sibling's, my wife's – it might even have been my own.

I began to walk across the savannah, alone now, my hands empty, the sky and the earth silent. My eyes looked out through my father's tears at a world of water and salt and sunset, a world of miscarriage, swelling, subsiding, and finally, breaking. Beside me, at once calm and filled with a savage power, walked the animal who would never be free, in any world, yet who turned the planet with its wanting. Far ahead of us, and never coming closer, the foetal curve of the horizon kept trying to be born, and the waters of the world broke red over the turning rock.

Dark, and Rain in the Air

. . .

MY DAD NEVER had any money, except for that time in Winnipeg, five years ago. He had been invited to read his poems at a university by an old friend of his who taught there. Anyway, that's not important. What's important is that Dad took us all – Mom and Win and me – with him on the trip, even though Mom said, "Winterpeg?" without laughing, and I saw Win frown where he was sitting at the kitchen table, eating Froot Loops.

Dad only sighed. "It's a change, Bess. We could use one."

Mom lit a cigarette and cinched her bathrobe tighter.

"You don't have to come. But the boys would miss you if you didn't. Wouldn't you, boys?"

Win just nodded slightly as he bent further over his cereal. I felt sorry for him, being as little as he was and still not really used to these sorts of talks. So I said from my chair across the table, "Yeah, Mom, we would."

She grinned at me and said, "That's a good boy, Jason. You back up your dad."

"Bess," Dad said quietly. He was standing against the apartment window, with the snowy, grey sky behind him. His white T-shirt wasn't much brighter than the sky, and the fly of his jeans was undone. He was always remembering about those jeans and zipping them up in public. Sometimes he'd smile and say, "Not time to let the cat out yet, I don't think." Which always made me and Win smile, though we'd heard it lots of times.

But now he didn't notice it. He just stood there, his big face blinking and his arms hanging at his sides.

After a while, when Mom just kept smoking, Dad said that we'd be staying in a nice big railroad hotel, all expenses paid, and that he'd get a nice fat cheque for the reading too.

Mom puffed out. She held up a stack of envelopes and fanned them loosely in Dad's direction.

He laid his heavy, unshaven face over to one side and, when Mom turned away, he winked at me and Win. I knew what he meant. He meant that she was going to come, and boy, won't we have a great time. I didn't really think so, but Dad was so cheerful about it, and Win too, that I tried to believe it.

Anyway, we took a plane to Winnipeg. It was Win's first time flying and he puked into a bag, so Dad rubbed Win's back and told him it was okay, lots of people got sick in airplanes. The stewardess was nice. She kept coming back to ask Win if he was feeling better. I figured I was lucky, getting to sit in another row beside two men in suits who didn't talk to me. I was reading *Danger on the Vampire Trail*, one of Dad's old Hardy Boys books that Grandma had sent us from Vancouver. "The man who wrote those books," Dad always said, "hardly saw a penny in royalties. And they've sold millions of copies. That man's son was a hockey broadcaster. I used to watch him on *Hockey Night in Canada* when I was growing up."

This sort of talk drove Mom crazy. She'd sigh heavily whenever she heard Dad come out with his "little Canadian facts." I was never brave enough to say that I loved them, but Dad knew it, so he never stopped telling me.

When we got to Winnipeg, it was really cold. We got into a taxi and Dad said it was like climbing into an igloo. The driver laughed and said that he'd give us some whale meat to chew on to keep our jaws from freezing. Dad and the driver got to talking, and we learned that the man was from Pakistan and that he'd just sponsored his wife to come over to Canada in the summer.

"Woman make a home," the man said cheerfully. "Man can't make a home. No good by himself. Just walls."

"Charming," Mom said.

The taxi driver didn't say much after that. But he smiled at Dad when the ride was over and thanked him very much for the tip.

As the taxi drove off, Dad encouraged us to look up at the hotel. It was terrific, really big and made of all this whitish sort of stone. I thought we might even find a train inside the lobby, there was so much room. But we didn't. Instead, when we went through the revolving glass doors, almost getting trapped, me and Win just stared at all the dark red carpet and the golden rails on the winding staircase and the big, shiny chandelier and the antique furniture and all the really huge oil paintings of trees and mountains, and all the hotel workers in these red uniforms almost as dark as the carpet.

Other guests stood around talking or sat in big leather armchairs smoking pipes and reading newspapers. I liked the smell of the pipes much better than the smell of Mom's cigarettes.

Win was staring up at the chandelier. "How come it doesn't fall?" he whispered to me. But Dad heard him and smiled.

"Don't you worry, Win. That's been up there nearly a hundred years. It's not about to fall on you."

We went to the desk and checked in. The man said we were in room 504, a non-smoking room, for three nights.

"Non-smoking," Mom said. "Non-smoking."

Dad blushed but didn't say anything to her. He just turned over the card the man gave him. It was our key. "How about that?" Dad said. I could tell he was really happy, just like he'd been the whole time since the Winnipeg trip came up.

"I feel like a character right out of an old movie," he said as we went through the lobby toward the gold staircase. "This is swank. And plush. Remember those words, fellas, and you'll always remember this place."

"But Daddy," Win said, screwing up his face, "I can't memember the last words."

Dad laughed. He was always telling us to remember words. But I knew he never really expected us to. He wasn't going to ask us later what they meant or anything. But Win wasn't old enough to know that.

Mom didn't want to come to the reading. She hardly ever came to them anymore. Instead, she said she was going to stay in the hotel lounge and make use of the expense tab.

"That's a good idea," Dad said with a big smile. "Enjoy yourself."

. . .

THE UNIVERSITY BUILDING was a big place with lots of hallways. Dad held Win's hand as we walked by all the students and took an elevator to the English department. In a place called the Faculty Lounge, which was kind of swank and plush but not like the hotel, we met Barry. He was about Dad's age, but short and round. He had a thick black beard and wore a green and blue T-shirt that said, "Friends of Clayoquot Sound."

"How goes the battle?" Barry grinned at Dad as he shook his whole arm. "It's been too long, too long."

Dad was grinning too. So was Win. And I figured I was too.

"Thanks for setting this up, Bar. We really needed a little holiday."

"Oh God, my pleasure, Drew, you know that." Then he looked at me and Win and winked.

Ten minutes later, after me and Win had heard about the summer Dad and Barry had fished Barry's dad's salmon boat, and how they were always getting into trouble with the tides because they had their noses buried in books, we arrived at the classroom where the reading would be.

There were maybe twenty people there by the time it started. Mostly they were students, but there were a few old people too, a couple even older than Dad and Barry. Dad was still in a good mood. After Barry said all sorts of nice things about him, things that made Dad put up his hands as if to say, "Oh stop," Dad stood at the front of the room and said he was really happy to be reading at the U of M. And he said it real slowly, then smiled, and said that U of M sounded so nice, like a Buddhist state of mind or maybe a yoga position. People laughed, but me and Win didn't get it. Of course, Win laughed anyway. He always did whenever anybody else did. He was always just like that. You had to love him for it.

Dad read mostly from his new book. I could tell the audience liked him, even if they didn't exactly understand him. But that was okay. Me and Win knew what that was like. And it didn't matter. Dad read the one about our great-grandma and the one about waking up in an old barn with animals all around and stars showing through a hole in the roof and the one I really liked about when he and Mom first knew each other and were visiting a friend in southern England where there were these big chalk drawings of naked people on the hills. Then, just at the end, he did something I'd never heard him do before. He said he was going to read a poem by the man he named his second child after. And then he asked Win to stand up. And Win did, laughing and smiling at everyone because they were laughing and smiling at him.

"This is a poem by Winfield Townley Scott," Dad said. "He's obscure but wrote very beautifully. I have always had a soft spot for him, because... well, there's something about obscurity and beauty that, together, almost define a poet's life." Then Dad took a deep breath and read the poem. All I remember about it is that there was a girl reading a book in an orchard and Dad wanted to speak with her, and then it was too late because when he tried to find her again, she was gone. And there was one line that Dad said maybe four or five times. "Dark, and rain in the air." I don't know why I remember that, but I do.

Dad finished reading and people clapped and then everybody left, except for me and Win and Barry and this pretty girl who bought Dad's book and asked him to sign it. She was one of Barry's students. Her name was Lianna, and she came to dinner with us. Win really liked her. And I did too. We all had a good time.

When we got back to the hotel, Mom wasn't in our room.

"She's probably enjoying herself downstairs," Dad said, then told us to read ourselves to sleep. He said they'd come up later, and that tomorrow we'd have a big fancy breakfast in the dining room.

Me and Win talked a bit, then he fell asleep. I read for a while, but I was too excited to stay in bed. I looked out the window at the city. Puffs of steam and smoke were coming up everywhere. Taxi cabs drove along the streets. I could see some really old buildings and some brand-new ones, and a sign that said "Try the New Vintage Casino." There was no moon or stars. At least I couldn't see any. I could hear the music from downstairs, and a woman singing. Finally, I just went to bed and fell asleep.

The next day, our last full day in Winnipeg, we all had breakfast together. Like Dad said, it was pretty fancy. The best part was when we got up to go to where these cooks in big white hats were standing and they asked you what you wanted and then they made it on this long stove right in front of you.

When we finished breakfast, Dad said he'd take us out to see the city. It wasn't as cold as yesterday, he said, and we could walk around, maybe buy something for ourselves. Mom said that she wasn't feeling well and would stay in the hotel. Dad looked quickly at her and opened his mouth and I thought he was going to say something. But he didn't.

I don't remember too much about our walk around Winnipeg except for the old brick buildings and the poor people. Dad couldn't stop talking about them. He kept stopping in the streets to the read the faded ads on the sides of the oldest buildings. And he must have given away ten loonies to poor people when they asked for change. Dad was always giving money to people in the streets. "There but for the grace of God," he'd say, because that was what Grandma and Great-Grandma said. In Winnipeg that time, Dad talked a lot about our great-grandma.

"Jason." He touched me on the shoulder when we stopped in front of some big old warehouse with grimy windows and signs that read "Office space for lease" in big block letters. "Your great-grandma probably lived in one tiny room in a building just like that. During the Great Depression. Her and your great-granddad and ten of your great-aunts and uncles." He shook his head, and a minute later gave a toonie to a long-bearded old man who smelled like beer.

I should have known right then that something bad was going to happen. The more we walked, the more dirty old buildings we stood in front of, the sadder Dad got and the more money he gave away. I was getting scared because I knew how upset Mom would be if Dad spent all of his reading money just like that. We went shopping and I had to try really hard to say that there was nothing I wanted just so Dad would keep his money in his pocket. Win didn't know any better, though. He got a remote-control car and a Bugs Bunny sweater. I whispered to him, "That's enough. Don't ask for anymore," and I think he understood what I meant. Win was pretty smart for four.

Dad didn't buy anything for himself, but he kept pushing stuff on me. "Come on, Jase, wouldn't you like this? Come on, you have to have something."

I didn't want to hurt his feelings, so I let him buy me a pair of Montreal Canadiens socks because they were in a bargain bin. I didn't say anything when he bought Mom this fancy, silvery-shiny blouse in a store that had mannequins with furs on them, even though I figured he bought it mainly to be nice to the girl who waited on us. Dad was always popular with girls.

So it's kind of strange that it was a girl who ruined our trip to Winnipeg. Well, I guess she ruined everything. But Dad said no, that she was just the straw that broke the camel's back.

Anyway, everything was going great. Mom said she'd had enough of the hotel and decided to come along for dinner with Barry and Lianna and us. And she was friendly too. She asked Lianna about her studies and told her she was so pretty that she'd have to watch out for her teachers. But mostly they all talked about books. They were really excited. Even Mom. She said that Dad ought to write novels, that he'd be good at it because even in his poems he was a born storyteller. And Barry and Lianna said yes, that was true, he was. And Mom said that nobody ever read poetry so you couldn't expect to make a living at it, and what was so wrong with being a man of letters anyway? Thomas Hardy, she said, figured all that out a hundred years ago. He wrote novels for money and wrote poems for love, after he'd made himself rich and famous. It's crazy to do anything else, Mom said, and Lianna excused herself to go to the bathroom. "An idealist," Mom sighed. "You fellas had better watch out, she's going to fall in love with you."

But nothing bad happened at dinner. It was all really nice. Mom even said so in the taxi back to the hotel.

And it was nice coming into the lobby, Dad with his favourite shirt and pants on, and some money in his pocket, and Win, sleepy now, up in Dad's arms, still staring at the big chandelier, and Mom stroking my hair and saying, "I wish I could pick you up in my arms like that, Jase. I would if I could," and then we went past the people talking and the piano music playing and into the elevator with the shiny brass doors and down the wide hallway to our room. And before I knew what was happening, me and Win were asleep and then there was a banging on the door and Dad was getting out of bed in the dark and flipping a light on and I looked at the clock radio and it was two o'clock and Mom was saying, "What is it? What's going on, Drew?"

I got up without waking Win and without Mom seeing me and went and stood as close to the door as I could. Dad had pulled it half-open and was standing blocking the light from the hall. A girl was crying, saying something about being ripped off, about the asshole next door, about some guy named Gordie who would kill her if she didn't bring back what she was supposed to get. She said this guy, Gordie, would blame her and not the john, and would beat her for it, and shit, what the fuck was she going to do, the bastard, the prick! I heard Dad say something soft. And then the girl, really loud, said she thought she was banging on the other guy's door, she was sorry, she was so fucked up, she didn't know what she was doing.

"Shhh," I heard Dad say, and then, "Come in here a minute and settle down."

Now Mom was up, and I had to hide just inside the bathroom door.

"Drew, what do you think you're doing? You can't bring her in here!"

"Bess, it'll be all right. She's been ripped off. She's scared." Then, in a whisper I barely heard, he added, "She's just a kid. Look at her."

But Mom didn't look at her. She just kept staring hard at Dad and shaking her head and saying "No, no, no. You get her out of here. Right this minute. Do you hear me? I'm not kidding, Drew. Right this minute. For Christ's sake!"

"Why not for Christ's sake?" Dad said, suddenly angry. He was hardly ever angry, so this kind of shocked Mom for a while. "If not for His sake, then whose?"

I looked at the girl. She was skinny and wore a thin black dress that had no sleeves. Her arms were really white, and there was a tattoo on her shoulder, but I couldn't tell what it was. And she had really long, really blonde hair; it was shiny, kind of like white fire. And her face was skinny except for her big lips which were almost as red as real fire. She was just crying now, and her skinny, white face was streaky and black.

"What's your name?" Dad asked, turning his back on Mom.

The girl said Sherry or Cherry, I couldn't quite tell.

"All right, listen. You stay here a minute and I'll see what I can do."

Dad left, and a few seconds later, I heard him knocking on the door next to us.

Mom didn't even look at the girl. But the girl stood with her head hanging down anyway, and sort of fell off her high-heeled shoes over and over, like it was a game she did to pass the time. I wondered how she did it. It was pretty neat, really, the way she rose up and then kind of slid her foot sideways so that it touched the floor without the shoe being on. The air smelled like perfume and cigarettes.

Dad came back quietly. "No surprise. He won't answer. And I suspect we won't see anything of him tomorrow. Gone with the sunrise, most likely."

"What am I going to do?" the girl said in a whiny voice.

"Get another line of work," Mom said. "Or go back to school." I could tell that she was really tired and that she didn't even think about what she was saying.

But Dad had lost his patience. "I think you'd better not say anything else, Bess."

I couldn't see Mom's face, but I guessed she was frowning as she quickly crossed the room to the window.

"How much?" Dad said quietly to the girl.

She screwed up her face and looked over at Mom.

"How much?" the girl repeated dully.

Dad sighed. "No, I'm paying for the guy next door. So you won't get into trouble with your... with Gordie."

For a few seconds the girl's mouth hung open. Then she said a hundred and something. I couldn't quite hear the exact amount. Then she stood there blinking as Dad counted out the bills into her hand.

"Oh God, thanks. This is amazing. I can't believe you're... why are you..."

Dad turned her to the door. He looked heavy when he moved. I'd never seen him move like that before. "Take care of yourself, all right?" he said, and lightly closed the door. Then he took off his clothes and got back into bed. About ten minutes later, when Dad started snoring, Mom got back into bed too. She'd been crying a little at the window and I really had to keep myself from going over to her. But I was glad I didn't, because it wouldn't have helped any. When I was sure they were both asleep, I snuck back to my own bed and got in beside Win, who had slept right through everything. And I laid there for a long time, hearing Dad's voice go all cold and hard, and I knew nothing was going to be the same again.

. . .

I DON'T HAVE much else to tell about Winnipeg. Mom and Dad weren't talking anymore, and me and Win mostly talked between ourselves. Dad tried his best to make things better for us. He told one of his little Canadian facts about this part of Winnipeg that the taxi went through. About a rock star growing up there, and how his band put out their first single and everybody bought it because they thought the Guess Who name meant it was really the Beatles playing on the single. I wasn't much into music then, but I think that's a pretty funny story now.

Anyway, Mom and Dad split up after Winnipeg, and me and Win lived with Mom some of the time and Dad some of the other. It was okay, but not like before. Then Dad was killed one night crossing the road to the store to get Win some ice cream and I thought we wouldn't be able to stand it, me and Win. We cried all the time. But probably you already know about Dad being hit by that car. After that happened, his books became sort of popular and people started calling up Grandma and Grandpa wanting to know all sorts of things about when Dad was a kid. And they called up Mom too, but she never answered anything.

Now, she hardly talks about Dad. She just says sometimes that he tried to carry the weight of the world on his shoulders but that nobody could do that, or even try, it was too big of a job. She's married again, to Eric. I like Eric okay, but that's not the same thing as loving him. Not loving somebody feels like . . . but I can't explain it. You'd have to be a poet like my dad was to explain something like that. But I sure know what it feels like. And Win does too. Dark, and rain in the air. That's what it feels like. It feels just like that.

This Is a Test of the Emergency Book-Buying System

. . .

IT RARELY GETS any colder on this planet. Forty below with wind chill and the experts on the radio are advising everyone to stay indoors unless it's absolutely necessary to go outside. But how do these experts – any experts – know what is absolutely necessary? They would say that brain surgery is a good reason to venture out – for patient and surgeon – any kind of medical emergency, of course, anything that's a matter of life and death. A funny expression, life and death. If there's breath and the heart beats, there's life. That's what the experts would say. The experts would also tell me to stay in and drink a cup of green tea and go over my investment portfolio and retirement plan. The experts would strongly advise me to listen to the experts. You will not die, they summarise in chorus, if you do not find a printed book by an American author named John Cheever that contains his famous story "The Swimmer." Stay in. Search when the deep freeze has lifted.

I have put on three layers – T-shirt, long-sleeved shirt, and sweater – and now I add a multicoloured wool jacket that I bought at Value Village a month ago, the fourth layer. Just like the four kinds of wood in the cross that they hung Christ up on. Olive, cedar, pine... I never remember them all. The toque I have just pulled on is older than me, and I'm old enough to still listen to the radio and to know how to spell toque. This one belonged to my father and it's grey with a bright orange tassel. He used to wear it out on the coast when he golfed in the winter, the only person on the whole course, standing on the soggy green like an ordinary seabird with one bit of exotic plumage.

The world outside my door is all Rembrandt etching of Goya bleak. I advance along the Munch bridge of the sidewalk under the cathedral-like, scorched-black boughs of the elms and listen to the mid-ocean creaks and groans in the Melville rigging. Not a soul in sight, and I count animals as creatures that have souls, if anything has souls. No birds. I'm as alone as whaleback on the pewter calm, which suggests there must be many experts on the internet as well. But the booksellers will be out, I know that. Or to be precise, they will have gone out in order to go in. Have you ever been a camel with a soul that has used every drachma of water in the hump and staggered on broken forelocks to an oasis? It's like that. For some of us, books are meat and bunker. They are a matter of... well, they matter.

I first read "The Swimmer" when I was twenty years old and used to swim a lot. In fact, I remember the exact reading occasion for that very watery reason. I had been working with my older brother, my only sibling, that summer as a swamper. In those days, Jeremy looked a fair bit like a young Jesus, all long-haired and long-bearded and bright-eyed and gold-skinned. Women of any age would have happily massaged his feet with olive oil. I was not attractive to the opposite sex – awkward, a loner, prone to stammering and blushing. My brother was only two years older than me, but he had the stoic self-confidence of a man in his forties. A full-time worker from the age of sixteen, he then drove a truck delivering liquor to Vancouver restaurants and nightclubs, and I swamped, which is to say helped to load and unload the goods. It was August, so hot you could taste the lemonades in the lemons that the children, who hadn't even had the idea to set up lemonade stands, hadn't even begun to slice. By late afternoon, we were shirtless and slick as newborns still in our cauls. We revolved as slowly as harbour seals under the sun. For extra income, my brother had a grass-cutting job in the wealthy district of West Vancouver, high on a bluff overlooking Howe Sound. He was irritable because he'd dropped an expensive bottle of wine and would have to pay for it himself, and so by the time we reached the eagle-eyrie mansions, I knew he had it in for the rich. That generally meant we had every right to their pleasures. In this case, that meant going for a swim in an hourglass-shaped swimming pool of gin-clear water that seemed somehow like a Turkish bath. Earlier, in the parking lot of the Blue Boy Motel, while I waited for my brother to straighten out invoicing with the manager, I read John Cheever's famous short story. It was on my fall course list. In those days, I was a university student with some vague idea of becoming a university professor.

Cheever's story is about a middle-aged man named Neddy Merrill who decides, one languorous summer day in the suburbs, to swim his way home via a sequence of backyard and community swimming pools. Through the course of his journey, he grows fatigued, the summer appears to turn to fall and then winter, and we learn that Neddy's life isn't exactly what he thinks it is. By the time he reaches his abandoned and locked house, it's apparent that he's lost everything – house, social standing, money, family. But I wasn't much moved by the point of the story at the time. Cheever's prose is so lyrical and rich, his evocations of sheer sensual pleasure so convincing, that reading "The Swimmer" only made me more grateful for my young body, the sunshine, and the gin-clear swimming pools of the privileged. That was probably Cheever's intention all along. But then, I never became a professor, and that reading is no doubt far too simplistic.

Thirty years later, my reading is the same, and different. Or I'm sure it would be if I had a copy of the story to read. And when I say "read," I mean in a book. And when I say "book," I don't mean electronic text. I mean book. There are times in a man's life when the desire to read a favourite story in the form in which he first encountered it is every bit as strong as a sexual urge or food craving. The same applies to music and painting and film. If this sounds odd or silly, I simply cannot help you, I cannot even see how to begin to help you.

The shreds of a "Lost cat" poster from two summers before flap in the wind as I pass a telephone pole. My breath is the size of the ghost of that cat, which was likely eaten by a coyote. I keep walking into that ghost, dissolving it, and creating another. By the time I've used up nine lives, I've reached my first stop. With luck, I won't need to make another. But when they were handing out luck, I thought they said flux, and that's where I've spent my whole life, happily and unhappily, as is the human lot, the swimming pools all clear and warm in summer, all empty and desolate in winter. Some people live better with one lung than most do who pretend to live with two.

The sign on the sidewalk reads *The Bookseller*, which used to be an amusing pun when the store was actually below street level. But now, since the move upstairs, the name is remarkably ordinary. The owner, however, is not so ordinary. Oh sure, when I enter, there's the standard classical music station playing on CBC Radio, which isn't really a classical music station – sort of the equivalent of farmed salmon to wild salmon. But you don't ever get straight AM radio in used bookstores, and pretty soon, of course, you won't get used bookstores. I read in a newspaper some years ago, the kind that you unfold like a limp seagull, the kind kids used to toss on doorsteps after they'd gone for a swim in the local community pool, that, at the turn of the century in England, there were three thousand antiquarian bookstores – a decade later, there were less than three hundred. By now, I guess there's some lone, cranky octogenarian Dickensian in the Cotswolds holding out like the last spotted plover against the cementing onslaught.

Fred Karsh isn't that old, and he brings to mind a more recent part of British culture. I'd guess he's in his early sixties, about six feet tall, pot-bellied, and – here's the Anglophilic point – sporting a mop top haircut that would make any Liverpool lad circa 1966 quite crown-proud. Except Fred Karsh's hair is as white as the moon. And his idea of popular culture ends at about William Wordsworth, though I did once hear him make a passing reference, almost in admiration, to Thomas Hardy.

I tell him now that I'm looking for John Cheever. Then I tell him who John Cheever is, or, rather, was – because Fred is unusual in that most of the books he sells don't interest him at all. The look I once saw him adopt as he held a copy of a Stieg Larsson novel would have chilled the blood of a tattooed vampire riding a dragon.

"American. Mid last century. Published a lot in the *New Yorker*. Stories dealing with post-WWII suburban life. Drinking, infidelity, financial loss. A rich, sensuous prose style."

Fred screws up his florid, rotund face and says "Popular?" exactly as if he is saying "Shit?"

"Oh, wildly so. Sold in the tens of millions. You know how much Americans love to read truthful examinations of the American Dream."

"Sarcasm," he replies grandly, "is from the Greek. It means 'to tear flesh.' In any case, I might have one of this fellow, Cheever's, tomes. But you'd be much better off with Hazlitt. When was the last time you read Hazlitt? Come to think of it, when was the last time you got any sleep? Or had something to eat? You can't…"

I cut him off, interested only in his first question about reading Hazlitt.

"This morning. At breakfast. With my Samuel Johnson porridge. I believe it was his essay, 'On Going a Journey,' in fact."

The bookseller smiles wryly and leads the way to his fiction section. Of course, I could simply have gone there myself without asking for help, but not every business is yet set up like a bank or an airline or a supermarket, with self-check-in, check-out terminals to eliminate the possibility of human interaction. Besides, it is a brutally cold day in the middle of a long Alberta winter – why should I deprive a curmudgeonly bookseller of the chance to mention William Hazlitt?

"Nothing by Sir Cheever," Fred Karsh announces, a little too proudly. "I do have a handsome edition of Keats's letters, though, if it's fine prose you're after. Most of the great poets wrote better sentences than today's so-called authors." He sniffs the musty air like some kind of golden retriever of culture. I half-expect him to drop to all fours and point his nose at the volume of Keats. Instead, without a word, he retreats behind his book-cluttered, barn-door of a computer-less desk. Fred Karsh relies on foot traffic not the internet for business, which explains why I am the only patron in the place. With intentional irony, I buy a handsome little edition of Arnold Bennett's *Riceyman Steps*, an early-twentieth-century novel about the troubles of a used bookseller. But the moptopped Karsh does not rise to the bait.

"O for a beaker of the warm south," he quotes at my back as the door swings shut behind me and a thousand meat lockers of cold slam into my face.

The line of Keats warms me for perhaps a half block. Then my whole spirit ices over. Just like a pool in Vancouver when a freeze hits before the pool is drained for winter. It's a ten-minute walk to Alhambra Books, and so I quicken my pace. After all, I don't want Roald Amundsen to get there first. Amundsen, Scott, and all those polar explorers would have appreciated "The Swimmer." The main character, as the professors like to emphasise, was on a quest. As am I. As are we all.

The cars speeding along the avenue are shrouded in white exhaust. But their engines and tires make so little noise that I feel I'm watching a funeral-procession-in-a-hurry. In general, it seems curious to ever be in a rush about anything, given our inevitable finish line. My brother always rushed. He routinely ran red lights on the job. I often had to close my eyes and just pray we wouldn't get hit. I wonder now why I bothered. Who doesn't get hit, early or late?

A police cruiser at the side of the road opens like a flower and out steps a female officer well over six feet tall. If I had any breath to spare, she would immediately take it away. Her partner slips out of the far side of the flower like a reluctant wasp. He's considerably shorter, probably just above the bar of the official minimum height requirements for the job. As I come abreast of the cruiser, I recall with piercing melancholy the vivid line of red paint on the brick wall beside the admission booth of the little community swimming pool in my hometown. Oh how I longed to rise above that red line so I could enter the pool by myself. What freedom! What a sense of expanding horizons! My pigeon-chest assumed a hawk-like proportion.

I smile at the Amazon officer and her Lilliputian partner, but they wear matching scowls and hold their hands at their revolver holsters as they approach the shuddering four-wheel drive they've just pulled over. The red siren light blinks fiercely, like the eye of the Cyclops after Odysseus has driven the burning log into it.

I plunge into Alhambra, from deep winter to intense heat, like a reverse move by one of those English kids in the Narnia books, going through the wardrobe. The owner, Scott Chadwick, owns more than ten thousand well-thumbed volumes of print; he also owns Alberta's largest heating bills. Some millionaire out of Chandler's *The Big*

Sleep could grow orchids between the sagging bookshelves of self-help tomes and *Harry Potter* reprints. Walking the slightly tilted floor is like patrolling the deck of a pirate ship at high noon off the sweaty coast of Madagascar.

Scott Chadwick is always disconcerting. Middle-aged, he has wild curly red hair and a wild thick red beard and full red lips. His smile's broad, his incisors pointy, fox-like. He speaks to me now out of the burning bush of his face, but his voice is anything other than godlike, unless God sounds like a shy teenage girl.

"You're a brave soul to venture out in this weather. Are you all right? I heard you've had some sad family news. Your nephew, was it? I'm so..."

I don't want to talk about Luke. Or even think about him. Talking and thinking bring his last words back to me, and I can't bear to hear them for the thousandth time. Better to be Neddy Merrill and keep right on moving. Maybe I didn't have the sensual delights of summer to buoy me up, but isn't it more appropriate to face the deepest human chill in the most frigid earthly temperatures? I close my eyes again on the image of Luke at the bridge railing and my ears on the sound of my brother's dying-of-cancer request that I would be his only son's guardian angel. Not much of an angel, in the end. Worse than... than... oh what was the clumsy angel's name sent to save Jimmy Stewart in that famous Christmas movie? Lawrence? No. Clarence? Yes!

I look up, exultant with successful memory.

"At least you don't have a self-check-out express lane for customers in a frenzy to read the latest Oprah selection before their book club meets in the church basement. Where else can a human being venture these days?"

The white sliver by the bookseller's eyes appears to vanish in the flames as he tilts his head like some monstrous robin to consider my comment. "Uh, yes... indeed. Oprah. Yes."

"She's never selected a book by John Cheever," I say, to help him out, as he is clearly discomfited by my social criticism. "Of course, he's been dead since the early '80s. 'The Swimmer' was published in 1964, the very year I was born. In *The New Yorker*, I believe. Or maybe it was in *Playboy*. Though that's not where I came upon it, nudge, nudge, wink, wink. You wouldn't have any Cheever, would you? Perhaps his *Collected Stories*?"

Scott Chadwick smiles in what looks like relief. The sweat stains under the armpits of his 1998 Folk Festival T-shirt are the size of Jupiter's moons, and darker. "I think I have something by Cheever," he says.

Together we trudge through the tropical heat to the appropriate shelf. He bends over as if he doesn't have a spine and comes up with a clothbound book in a frayed dust jacket.

"Oh, sorry, it's a Susan Cheever."

He puts one hand to his face and the fire devours it. Then, miraculously, like a dove, his hand flies free.

"The daughter," I explain. "Also a writer. She inherited her father's drinking problem, if not quite his literary gift. But she tried, bless her. And succeeded too, after a fashion. Wrote several books. No shame in that. One must try."

Sweat stings my eyes and feels thick as blood around the edges of my toque. I pluck a little tear of sweat off my cheek. It's as clear as gin, as clear as the waters of that Gatsby-like swimming pool where Jeremy and I stripped naked and bobbed up and down like beer bottles while a raven chuckled throatily in an evergreen and the sky was such a pure azure that the passing airplanes might have been salmon. Jeremy was just in his early twenties then, and, despite his work ethic and self-assured demeanour, still had a firm claim on youthful excess. How many times I had to get out of the truck and go into a nightclub or restaurant and pry him away from the daytime waitresses and female managers – or maybe I should say maenads? Well, if something's going to tear you to pieces, why not women? That's a human danger, at least.

"You're right about that," the burning bush says, and I'm not sure whether he's referring to my comment on trying or to my thoughts about women. It doesn't much matter. "The Swimmer" isn't to be found here, so it's time to move on. I have one final stop before resorting to the chain stores. After that, it'll be the public library. But I want to own the story, I want to have it on my bedside table at the height of summer, when some quality in the pine-scented air or the prow-like shape of an approaching thunderhead makes my whole body feel like a vigorous comma in one of Cheever's magnificent sentences.

Hoar frost settles in delicate, pale insects on my eyebrows and eyelashes as I stagger into the steel trap of the wind. The fashionable quarter of the city lies just ahead, its bars and restaurants and cafés all curled up together like a pack of sled dogs. I can almost taste that furry warmth, that particular mahogany flavour of a midday drink. Not Samuel Hearne, not Alexander Mackenzie, not any bandy-legged European snowshoeing toward a fort of timber and the wisdom of the locals ever knew a greater thirst than I know as I fall against the door of The Title Page and then almost collapse like a gut-shot polar bear onto the ample bosom of one of the shop's two owners.

"Good God, man," says Camilla Dupre, "you look as if you've been out walking for hours." Camilla is either an operatic blonde diva or a female wrestler, depending on her mood. Today, she seems uncertain, caught between personas. A kind of doughy maternalism squeezes out and holds me tight until I regain my balance and composure.

"I'd offer you a brandy," she continues in a hushed voice, "but I realise that's not a good idea."

Suddenly, Camilla's partner, Linda, emerges from behind a shelf and clears her throat. She's a medium-sized brunette with medium-length brown hair and a medium-toned voice who likes to wear cat's eye sunglasses indoors, all year round. I suppose she suffers from migraines, but I've never been bold enough to ask her. Linda manages the shop rather the way that Margaret Thatcher managed England. But that was some time ago. I try for several seconds to think of the current English prime minister. Then I realise that I've never known it. At a certain point, exactly when I can't remember, I had taken Schopenhauer's advice and stopped reading newspapers.

Camilla gently pries the copy of *Riceyman Steps* from my hands, which resemble lobster claws, they are so large and brightly gloved. She ushers me towards a chair while casting a disapproving look at her life and business partner. Seconds later, the two are whispering fiercely. It's as if two of Macbeth's witches have decided to plot against the third. Still standing, I almost drift off. In fact, I might have dozed briefly. The chemical tang of chlorine snaps me awake. A phone rings like a bell buoy. Jeremy, treading in the deep end, suddenly grows more serious than usual.

His Nordic face turns Moorish. I hear him ask me to promise him something, something a man of his age shouldn't even think to ask. "If anything ever happens to me," he says, "you'll promise to look after my family, won't you? If I ever have any kids, I mean? You'll make sure to step up?"

I nod with the blazing doubloon of the coastal sun almost blinding me and the quivering shadows of the evergreens stretching their freestyles across the clear waters. Why else should that warm depth turn ice cold if I hadn't heard the clap of doom in my brother's voice, a sound that would take almost a quarter century to finally explode?

"He's obviously not well," I hear a grim voice say. All the books in the shop shift like crows, flap their jacket wings. It is still a sinister Scottish moment. The voice continues. "There must be someone we can call. Look at him. He's on the point of a stroke. And he's been drinking."

A stroke! A stroke! Ha! One more of those and I'll reach the edge of that rich man's pool and pull my young body out and use it to prevent the future from happening to my blood, my blood which so far shows no sign of cancer. I even pointed the fact out to Luke on that last phone call. He had said, "Both of my parents dead of cancer in their forties, and you think I should look after myself better?" With my usual cleverness, I responded, "In a game of Russian roulette, not every Russian dies from the bullet. Maybe there's no science in it, but I like to think that those tragedies are the end. That you'll have a long and rich life." I couldn't see the mocking pain in his face, but his tone vibrated with it. "Yeah? I thought bad things happened in threes." "That's not scientific either," I said. Then he pleaded for me to send him more of his money again, money that I knew he'd just use to keep harming himself.

I told him to wait. That I just had to tie up a few loose ends at work and then I'd come to the coast and we could talk things over in person. "Ok, Unc, you take care of what you need to do. I'll see you sometime." As clever as I am, I didn't hear the grave mystery in the last word my nephew ever spoke to me, or perhaps to anyone. I just didn't hear it, though the sound was a Russian gunshot. Are the surviving roulette players meant to feel relief? I felt only horror.

"Never, never, never, never, never," I think, or possibly say. I can't be sure. But there's a sympathetic woman's face hovering in front of me, so I go on with the King Lear quotations. "Why should a dog, a horse, a rat, have life, / And thou no breath at all?" I smile at the frowning woman, or try to smile.

"You really need to sit down," Camilla or perhaps Linda says. "Or you can lie on the couch in the office. That's probably a very good idea."

Thinking immediately of a horizontal body, I can't, as I have so often done, keep playing the fool. "Can you... can you imagine... have you ever had to go to the morgue?" The tears blur my vision even more, as I try to swim through them but find only other water. "I remember one day, when he was only four or five, he was playing in the puddles in the street. In shorts and bright yellow gumboots. Such a round, smiling face. And those blue eyes! A neighbour lady, walking by, said, he's so cute, he's as bouncy as a beam of sunlight."

I look up but can't see anything except shifting wet colours. My voice carries on despite my flawed vision, however. "What kind of fate is it that a man, a weak and careless man, should have to identify a beam of sunlight in the morgue?"

"You can't blame yourself," one of the women says. "Often there isn't anything that a person can do to help someone else."

"I just remembered. The fool in Lear. What he often calls the king. Nuncle." I suddenly make a Shakespearian decision to remove the fool from the stage. Besides, I see no sense in asking about the Cheever here. This is more of a Virginia Woolf sort of bookshop. Woolf, who also died by her own hand, in water.

All at once, the temperature is decidedly chill, even though the hoar frost has melted off my eyelashes and my lips are as numb as if I've been stung by a hornet. I force the blood through my legs and make for the door.

"Hey! Wait!" Camilla cries, but I hear the female wrestler in her tone and do not turn back. I run, gasping, heaving breath-clouds like sputtering, backfiring wand spells, and come within minutes to the revolving glass doors of one of the chains, a Quartos or a Chapters or an Indigo Folios.

I push inside, but not before catching a terrible glimpse of myself in the glass. I look like one of those sailors from Franklin's doomed expedition dug up out of the perma-frost – sallow, savage-grinned. And the vast space in which I find myself has a piercing Arctic glare. Shelves of glossy fashion magazines and tables piled head-high with bargain hardcovers and new releases whirl around me like polar bears smeared with neon lipstick. Then I calm myself and see that I'm in a new car lot, that the tables and shelves are offering me the latest models to test-read. Faintly relieved, I lean on a stack of self-help manuals and wait until the evenly controlled heat thaws my cheeks and jawbone. A hundred yards away, a red-uniformed employee gazes into a computer terminal. Something faintly alt-country plays out of hidden speakers. Just to my left, the vast space opens onto a franchise coffee shop named after a character in *Moby-Dick* who just wanted to collect his money and go home. Several young people sit at tables, their heads dripping with white cords, their faces bathed in faint cellphone and computer light. I can't smell anything, not even coffee. I drag myself, like the carcass of a grizzly on its own grease, to the distant employee and ask my familiar question.

He looks at me out of incredibly bright, young, blue eyes. His name tag reads "Skyler." I have never met a Skyler before. In half a century of life, not one single Skyler. This strikes me as incredibly sad as I follow the straight-backed, clean-browed boy to the fiction section and receive the familiar reply. No John Cheever. No books by this man who'd started a novel about a middle-aged swimmer in the suburbs and then condensed one hundred pages of notes down to a single short story. All that struggle, all that creative instinct, and "The Swimmer" might as well have never been written.

"You should download it off Amazon," Skyler says. And it occurs to me: wasn't there a character from the Muppets named Skyler? Or maybe it was Fraggle Rock? Had someone my age named their child out of nostalgia for shows peopled by puppets? "We don't have this author," Skyler continues, "but there's got to be an e-book of his out there."

"E-books aren't actually books," I say. "Books are books. Maybe you mean electronic texts."

Skyler isn't being paid enough to put up with my attitude. He shrugs as I blink. Somehow, when I see him again, he's rising on an escalator. It's almost glorious, like a Renaissance painting. The Ascension of Skyler into Children's Books and Merchandise. I say to his vanishing back,

"Please. I would have given you all your money. My own money too. Please. I really didn't know. Luke. Just wait. I'll be there."

But by then my vision has blurred again and I realise I need to go to the bathroom. Badly. For several minutes, I wander around like an acned employee, only minus the acne, until finally I find a door with a little white figure on it, just like at a crosswalk, the ghostly figure of a man about to dive into a pool. But when I hurl myself against the door, my wrist almost breaks. Locked! I gaze desperately behind me. Where is Skyler with the key? Openly crying now, I lean against the implacable barrier, my cheek against the little swimmer, poised forever like my brother, now also high on the railing of the Lions Gate Bridge, gazing down at the moment that I cannot keep my promise to protect his son. I can hear water running but I can't see it or smell it or touch it. And then I am very high above the vanished summer, with a God's-eye view of two dark shapes in a clear pool, two eaglets in the eyrie without protection from wind or light. Farther below, a ferry leaves the Sound. It does not look like a slice of wedding cake. It looks like an organ removed from a healthy body. It looks like the twenty-first century and I do not want to descend to it and stand at the railing with all the other sad figures. But already I feel myself falling, like a swimmer, like a man diving through to the fathom of his heartbeat, into the false waters that cleanse nothing and no one and reflect only a wintry sky.

Sidelines

. . .

"STAND RIGHT HERE, Ken. No! Here, here!"

Dad took me by the shoulder, gently but not as gently as when the day had started several hours ago. Then, the sun had been shining and we were all filled with a curious sense of adventure. Now banks of black cloud broke the sky and a light slanting rain had begun to fall. We were bored, hungry and cold, especially Janice and Tony. But Dad, if anything, was even more excited than he'd been when we'd boarded the ferry at Gibsons; he kept lifting his face to the rain and smiling, as if the weather had consented at last to participate in his plans.

"Okay, Tony, you be in goal this time. Stand a little off the line and take a couple of steps towards Ken when I give the word."

Dad turned and bent at the waist to speak to Janice. He wore only a thin white T-shirt, a Stanfields, which was what his own father had always worn. In a good, expansive mood, Dad would sometimes tell us about Robert Stanfield, the underwear man who'd run for prime minister and lost one election partly because a photographer took a picture of him bobbling a football.

But Dad's mood wasn't so jolly on this day; in fact, it was still a mystery to us, as much of a mystery as his actions. He'd always been fond of telling stories from his past, but he'd never taken us physically to the place of his exploits. I couldn't quite get over a rising sense of dread, even though, for the moment, Dad remained cheerful enough.

"I'm hungry," Janice whined. "I want something to eat."

Dad pushed her lightly into position between me and Craig.

"I'll get you something soon, honey. Just stand here. Okay, now..."

He rubbed his hands together and, backing slowly away from the goal, addressed us.

"On this field, on a day just like this one, I scored not one, not two, but three – yes! three! – goals off corner kicks. Each one a header too. And look at me, a half inch over five foot eight."

He chuckled and shook his head. Then he removed his glasses and wiped the rain from the lenses.

"We were playing an Italian team we'd never played before. When I scored the first goal, it was no big deal. But once I scored the second, oh boy. There was this huge guy – Rocco or Gino or something – hairy as a gorilla, and he was assigned to mark me, to follow me all over. But on that last corner kick, I swear I had half of Little Italy hemming me in. It was a real crush, lots of elbows and cursing."

Dad sighed. His chest hair showed like the pelt of a small animal as the rain darkened his T-shirt.

"I floated then, kids. You should have seen me. I wish you could have been there. They couldn't have stopped me if the Pope himself had issued a special decree."

He turned towards the corner of the field and raised his hand.

"Watch, now. I remember I started my run from about twenty-five yards out. Dean Jesperson took the kick, curved it in. Okay, Tony, move out a bit. I cut to my left... Ken, put your arm out to grab me, that's right. Craig, you jump when I give the word. Okay, go!"

Dad moved around Janice, I kept my arm out, Craig jumped, Dad snapped his head forward at the imaginary ball, Tony looked lost, and five seconds later it was all over.

"Funny thing is," Dad said sadly, catching his breath, "we lost four to three. But still, it was something. Three goals, all headers. Those Italians couldn't believe it."

It was up to me again, as the oldest.

"What happened the next time you played them?"

Dad's eyes scanned the grey horizon, as if the ball he'd scored with nearly thirty years before could be found there. But now his glasses streamed with rain, and he didn't remove them. The seconds passed heavily. A seagull shrieked and dropped like a stone behind a frayed bank of poplars. The sound of traffic – like a rushing creek – came from the highway. It was late September and in a few hours it would be dark. I had no idea how long Dad was going to keep this up. We'd already been to three other fields – one surrounded by subdivisions and a mall, one just under the Lions Gate Bridge where Dad's team had won an all-star tournament, and one in a wooded area near the university. Now we were somewhere in East Vancouver in the pouring rain, waiting for Dad's response. When it seemed that he hadn't heard my question, I repeated it.

He ran a hand through his wet hair and a long shudder passed through him.

"I don't know, Ken. Maybe it was the only time we played them. I don't remember."

His voice dropped like the gull, except without sound.

Cautiously, Craig stuck the earplugs for his iPod back in. Not a good idea, I thought, but he was only twelve, and I'd have done the same at that age.

But Dad didn't take any notice, though Craig had the volume turned up so loud it was easy enough to recognise the song. Rap. The worst possible choice. "Middle-class white kids wanting to be disenfranchised Black kids," Dad liked to say. "O brave new world that has such creatures in it." But he said nothing this time.

Janice repeated that she was hungry, and Tony complained that he was cold. Only I seemed to sense where we were headed next, and why Dad had fallen silent. I didn't exactly understand his silence, though, or where it was leading, and not knowing scared me. Yet I couldn't bring myself to ask. I just couldn't.

Finally, the rain fell hard enough to shock Dad back to his senses.

"All right, kids, let's go."

He walked away as if every drop of rain added an ounce to his weight. He seemed to sink into the grass. I tried as hard as I could to imagine him as a young man in a soccer uniform floating towards the goal amongst a group of cursing Italians. But the day had turned too miserable for me to imagine anything.

Fifteen minutes later, we crossed the Fraser River, at its north arm, which was like a thick strip of the gloomy sky brightened only by some log-booms the colour of Irish-setter fur. Dad, hunched over the steering wheel, looked neither to the right nor left. Soon we entered the deeper darkness of a tunnel and plunged under the river's south arm. Janice reached over from the back seat and pulled at my shoulder. I knew what she wanted to ask, but I had warned all three of my siblings on the ferry ride over not to bother Dad. And Mom, I discovered later, had done the same the night before. All she had said to me, however, was, "Keep an eye on him, Ken. He's not used to driving. Make sure he's paying attention."

I looked at him now, at his small, neat hands clenched on the wheel so tightly that the bones at the back stood out sharply. His cheek was grizzled, his jawline firm but with the beginnings of a second chin starting to show. It was a profile I'd never studied so intently, and I was surprisingly moved. Tears filled my eyes and I turned away to look out my window just as we reached the exit to the little fishing town where Dad had grown up and where most of his favourite triumphs – as well as failures, for he seemed to revel in them just as much – had occurred. I loved the place, but it had been years since I'd seen it. Our grandmother had left seven or eight years before, to live with our aunt and her family in Ontario, and so there'd been no reason to return. I doubted that Craig, the next oldest, even remembered the town. And I certainly wasn't going to ask him, not now, not with Dad suddenly tapping on the wheel with one hand while looking more out his window than through the windshield.

By the time we reached the large complex of soccer fields behind an elementary school, the rain was crashing down, the clouds like bits of wet plaster. A shabby playground consisting of a jungle gym of old tires and knotted ropes, some grey teeter-totters and a tetherball with a rock-like ball stuck to the end of an iron chain stood between the school and the first set of goalposts. The grass of the field was sparse, a dull, slick green. A couple dozen crows picked away at the soggy remains of some kid's abandoned sandwich. It was late afternoon, probably close to supper, and there wasn't anyone around. Dad had given us ball caps and told us to zip up our coats, but otherwise he seemed oblivious to the weather. He didn't even put on his own coat.

"We always played in the rain," he said, and stopped at the edge of the eighteen-yard box, which was only a faint burnt line on the ground. I wondered if anybody ever played soccer here anymore. One of the crossbars had a sag in the middle and there were large patches of dirt shining like picked scabs all over the field. "And in the middle of winter too. Cold! You have no idea. One time, when we were about fourteen, Oliver Bradley took a shot right on the thigh. No sweatpants allowed then. If we played, we played in shorts, and not even the goalies wore gloves. Anyway, it was so cold that Oliver cried. His face and his thigh were beet-red. That was the only colour in the game."

But Dad's mood wasn't as light as his words; it had grown heavier and darker with the day, as if the day had passed into him.

"He died before he even reached forty. Of cancer. Little Oliver Bradley. Right there, just beside where you're standing, Craig. I can see him plain as day. Crying and trying so hard not to. We were fourteen, you see. You're not supposed to cry at fourteen. Right there he was standing."

Dad walked over and stood beside Craig.

"And what's changed? What's changed? Only time. That's all. Nothing but time. If he had stood there, crying or not crying, and let the years come to him..."

Janice started to cry herself now, not because she understood – none of us did, really – but because she could tell that something had changed in Dad; it was as if several bones of his skeleton had simply turned to dust. Craig, probably because of what Dad had just said about being fourteen, tried to look cool, unaffected, but I could tell by the way he fiddled with the rim of his cap that he was faking it. Tony, as Tony always did, responded to emotion with open affection. He ran up to Dad and hugged him tight around the waist and buried his face in Dad's soaking wet T-shirt. I thought that would solve things. The two of them, in all that rain, on that empty field, looked like the last two survivors on the deck of a sinking ship, except it seemed that everything else was sinking around them. I expected Dad to shake himself out of his dark reveries and respond to Tony's love exactly like the father he'd always been. Instead, he cried out:

"Don't! Just don't!"

Then he pried Tony's arms apart and shoved him onto the grass.

"Hey!" Craig said. "What are you doing? You can't..."

"Shut up! Just shut up! All of you. You're useless. You're no goddamn good to me at all."

Dad breathed so hard that he was panting; his shirt was so wet it looked blood-soaked. Rain streamed down his face, and I doubted he could even see us through his blurred lenses.

"You're supposed to make a difference. But it's a lie. The biggest lie going. You make no difference. Do you hear me? None! It's just as hard, just as cold. None. No difference. None."

He turned and kicked savagely at the ground, losing his balance but righting himself again. His voice was quieter but still shaking.

"I scored here almost every Saturday from the time I was six until I was eighteen. Hundreds of goals. Hundreds!"

He took off his glasses and hurled them at the goal-posts. They made no sound when they landed. When he turned back to us, it was as if a layer had peeled off his face. Now he looked both young and old, like a boy swimming up through the man's bones. I wasn't shocked anymore, I was scared. I had picked Tony up to comfort him and now hugged him to me so hard that he gasped. But he didn't push away. Even Craig had stopped his act and let Janice cry against him; his hand rested awkwardly on the top of her head. I could see that his own shock was turning to anger. But he was twelve; it was to be expected.

"And she saw every single one," Dad continued, as if challenging someone other than us to deny it. "Every one. No matter how cold or wet it was. She stood here, on these sidelines, and she cheered. She cheered for me and she cheered for little Oliver Bradley and she even cheered for the other team when they made a nice play. When I phoned her and told her that Oliver had died, do you know what she said? She said, oh he was such a sweet boy, bless his heart."

He wasn't seeing us now; I didn't know who he was seeing or who he thought he was talking to. Without his glasses, the field would have been a grey blur and we would have been shadows, vague shapes to move from one year to another, and himself wandering heavily among them. His voice suddenly weakened.

"Who says that nowadays? Bless his heart? Who blesses anyone's heart?"

He started to shake. All the rain he'd taken into him all day had reached his bones at once. His teeth chattered.

There was no mistaking his tears for the rain anymore; his tears might as well have been blood, they were so clear. He looked very small.

It was up to me again. I waited until I was sure our grandmother's shade had blessed his heart once more, and not for the last time; I knew there would never be a last time. Then I walked over and gently placed my brother's warm body into our father's open and repentant arms.

The Key of Life

. . .

I COME FROM A large Irish Catholic family, of whom only one member, my Great-Uncle Francis, is an atheist. He's also the only one who collects contemporary art and suffers from clinical depression. My father doesn't come right out and say so, but I've always picked up the subtle suggestion that he believes my uncle's mental illness is connected to his atheism. I'm not sure he includes the art collecting in that connection. No one in the family likes to talk about the art, partly because they lack any capacity for doing so and partly because much of it – the conceptual and meant-to-shock stuff – embarrasses them. In any case, even at twenty, I understood that the situation was much more complex than my father's hints acknowledged.

I love my uncle – we've always enjoyed each other's company – and so I wasn't annoyed or, frankly, much surprised when my father, sensing trouble in the first few months of the pandemic, deputised me as a secret guardian and spy.

"Just tell him you're a little bored and would like to get out more," my father said. "He'll be sure to ask you along on one of his... outings."

The stress on the last word was mysterious but not alarming, at least not to me. "Outing" in our family could mean anything from having coffee with a fellow non-believer to visiting a gallery of contemporary art to buying drugs off a dealer in some darkened box-store parking lot. And to be honest, I was a little bored, a little too reliant on screens to occupy my time – it didn't help that all my university courses had gone virtual – and so any of these three options was welcome.

"You won't need that, Tommy boy," my uncle said as I climbed into his beat-up Ford Explorer, which puffed away like a woolly mammoth in the still wintry April air. "We won't be stopping. At least not for long. Most everything's closed tight as a banker's fist anyway."

I took off my mask – quite happily, as I still wasn't used to wearing it – and settled back for the drive, wherever it would take us. My boredom was such that I preferred the mystery. In fact, I was trying to let myself accept that I was more than bored; I was anxious, even lost. I just wasn't convinced that my life was heading in the right direction.

We drove north, across the river, to one of Edmonton's more depressed neighbourhoods. The streets were eerily empty, something that I hadn't grown accustomed to. Uncle Francis, as always, liked to play his music loud, and now he had on one of his favourite albums: Stevie Wonder's *Songs in the Key of Life*. My friends often turned to me for musical recommendations, and most of my old-school education in that area began and ended with my uncle. My parents certainly weren't going to introduce me to hard bop jazz or English ska.

"I think you two will really hit it off," Francis said. He turned his great shaggy-bearded, sunken-eyed face to me and winked. "Otherwise, I wouldn't let your father get away with his shenanigans."

"Shenanigans?"

"Now, Tommy, I know that under this wild beard I have the cheeks smooth as the proverbial baby's bottom. Nonetheless, I wasn't exactly born yesterday."

"It's a weird time," I said. "He only wants to make sure you're okay."

Francis thumped the steering wheel so hard that I flinched.

"He's only wanting to stick his nose into my business, as usual, the sancti... ah, never mind." The shift from outrage to calm was, I had to admit, so swift as to be unsettling. "Any reason to see more of you, my boy, is plenty reason enough. Do you know, after all these years, I still never remember the title of this song. 'Sir Duke.' I always think it's called 'Feel it All Over,' because of the chorus. Oh well. It's a nice tribute to Duke Ellington. I wonder what he thought of it. Maybe you can Google that for me while you wait."

With that, he braked outside a standard two-storey apartment building that looked like one of the winter's last snowmen – dirty and dissolving – and shambled off into the shredded glow of a streetlamp.

I took out my phone and started to read about the "Sir Duke" song. But before I got very far, my uncle returned, but not alone. He had a woman with him. Much to my surprise, and, admittedly, discomfort, she opened the passenger-side door and started to climb in, forcing me to unbuckle and slide over. I think the scent coming off her would have been enough to pick me up and move me. It wasn't unpleasant, but it was powerful, and put me in mind of a mix of incense and freshly turned soil. In the end, the scent didn't matter, because the woman herself, in appearance and manner, was so striking.

She had long lustrous blood-red hair spilling away under what was obviously a homemade pastel toque, and her face, porcelain-white and beginning to crackle around the eyes, was – how can I say this? – movie-star beautiful. I mean, she had to be approaching fifty, and I just wasn't used to seeing women of that age who were so stunning, at least not close-up anyway.

I glanced at my uncle, who seemed to be rubbing his hands with glee even though his hands on the steering wheel weren't moving. He was at least two decades older than this woman, and, to the best of my knowledge, had never been a ladies' man. In fact, I had never really thought of him, or of any people past a certain age, as having a romantic life.

"Bound to be slim pickings now, Charlie, wouldn't you think? Oh, Tommy, this is Charlie."

The woman, also, like my uncle, without gloves, shook my gloved hand.

"Ah, the university student. Very pleased to meet you. What exactly is it you're studying again? Francis did tell me. Math, is it?"

"Engineering," I managed to say, despite being plunged into a whirlwind of sensations, both pleasurable and disturbing. I simply wasn't used to being in such proximity to female beauty, no matter what age.

"Ah yes, bridges and the like. Important work. Do you like it?"

I shrugged, feeling more and more boyish. "It's okay."

The woman, leaning across me so that her vivid hair brushed my cheek and her scent wafted even more powerfully, spoke to my uncle with a mixture of enthusiasm and reassurance.

"Oh, I don't know about slim pickings. The truckers are still on the move. And they do most of the damage anyway."

"Right enough," Francis said, and increased our speed, the old Ford rumbling and rattling under the sound of the vintage music. "Terrible, of course. Terrible, but..."

She laughed – and it was the sound of ice clinking in a summer pitcher of lemonade. "Yes, I'm always half-hoping that we'll fail." She sighed. "But we mostly seem to find something, alas."

By the time we were on the Trans-Canada, heading west towards Jasper, I understood what we were meant to be doing. That is, I understood in a basic sense. We were looking for roadkill. And we were looking for it because this woman, Charlie (not short for Charlotte, she explained, but just Charlie, because her father had loved Roald Dahl so much), was an artist who used roadkill in her work. That was the part I was still puzzling over when the Catholic boy in me noticed something he really would have been better off not noticing: the wedding ring on her finger. And that in itself wouldn't have been significant if I hadn't also picked up on the obvious chemistry – yes, that kind of chemistry – between Charlie and my uncle. Hurtling through the pale darkness towards Hinton, on an almost-deserted highway, I was already planning what not to tell my father. The truth was, I'd spent much of the past few years planning what not to tell him. My lack of interest in engineering, for example. My increasing disinterest in religion. My longing to escape from what felt like a narrow and judgmental world where ritual wasn't so much a way to celebrate life's beauty as a way to shut it out. We had been close when closeness was easy: stopping at Tim Hortons after my hockey games, or hiking and camping in the Rockies. But now, it already seemed obvious that my uncle and his friend would be more receptive to my doubts and my longing to travel a different path. Somehow the pandemic made everything in my life smaller and more hopeful at the same time, even if I didn't know exactly how that hope would play out.

It was a moonlit night, and so the pavement ahead of us and even the stunted tree lines farther back from each side of the road were clearly visible. My uncle, singing along with the music, drove, as he always did, with great care and confidence. Charlie, meanwhile, sat far forward, peering through the windshield, and only after a while did I understand that she wasn't wearing her seat belt.

An hour passed before my uncle, stopping the music, said, "There," and reduced his speed. A black smear widened as we approached. Charlie jumped out of the truck almost before it had completely stopped, and my uncle quickly followed. I had no real interest in roadkill, but I was curious about how it figured into anyone's art, as I liked to draw pictures myself in my spare time. Eager to hear their conversation, I joined them in the hushed icy air.

Wreathed in breath-clouds, we stood without speaking for half a minute over the splayed-flat carcass of a large raven. It must have been dead and driven over for many days and looked – I couldn't help noticing – with its wings extended as if it had been crucified.

"Poor thing," Charlie said, and went down on one knee to touch the bird's crushed head. "Ravens don't usually die this way."

"At least it would have been quick." Francis spoke with a reverence that I rarely heard in his voice. "Not like some of the larger creatures."

Charlie nodded and ran her gloveless right hand along one of the raven's crushed wings. I couldn't be sure, but I thought she might have been on the verge of tears.

Francis knelt beside her. "I'm sorry. I didn't think. I mean, I thought that you'd faced up to the worst of all this by now."

She turned quickly towards him. "Contrary to popular opinion, Francis, you need a thin skin and not a thick one to be an artist. How else is anything meaningful going to get in?"

"Of course, you're right. But you see, my dear, I am not an artist."

The passion that now flooded into her voice would have embarrassed me if the passage of a giant rig speeding by in the opposite direction hadn't drowned out the ensuing silence.

"Oh, but you are! You know that you are. You've always been."

Once the silence had returned, Uncle Francis gently placed the raven inside a clear plastic bag. We returned to the truck, its emergency lights blinking like the eyes of panicked animals, and Francis put the bag in the back. We'd stopped for a full five minutes, yet only the one semi-trailer had rushed by. It was so strange. In fact, even more strange than what we had been doing. I couldn't help but feel that somehow the whole world was crouched at the side of the highway, waiting.

Every night for the next two weeks, I accompanied my uncle and his artist friend on these roadkill adventures.

In that time – and I wish I could say this without embarrassment – I too fell for Charlie, whose genuine sorrow for the slaughtered animals was as saintly as anything I'd encountered. Plus, her passion for turning that sorrow into art was as attractive as it was infectious. Eventually, I was bold enough to ask her directly why she had come to care so much for these gravel-encrusted and mangled victims. We were in the warehouse in the oil refinery district that my uncle rented to store his surplus art collection – he also rented a corner of the vast space to Charlie as a studio (she insisted on paying him). While he was out to get the thermos of coffee he'd left in his truck, she told me, in a voice that now struck me as exhilaratingly confidential, and which echoed all around the high-ceilinged and mostly empty space, that, as a woman, and particularly one who had been in a very bad relationship for many years, she naturally empathised with any form of life that fell victim to power and violence.

"My husband, you see. Well, to be direct about it, isn't a good man."

"He's a brute is what he is."

My uncle, stomping snow off his boots, wore a rare look of disgust on his normally beaming face. "Violent. He hit her, Tom. Kicked her pets too."

I noted my uncle's use of the past tense but didn't register what that meant. Charlie still wore her wedding ring, but I realised that she couldn't likely spend every evening with my uncle if she was still living with her husband, especially not during lockdown, when everyone was staying home so much.

"I finally talked her into leaving him," Francis explained, as if reading my mind. "But he won't agree to a divorce, the bloody hypocrite. There's your Catholic religion, Tommy. In a nutshell. Weekday sinner and Sunday saint, my mother used to say."

"Now, Francis, you shouldn't be saying such things to . . ."

"Oh, Tommy's heard all my sacrilege many times. It's old news to him. There is no God, and Mary is his mother. All that." He turned to me, a sort of pleading in his eyes. "But I've never proselytised, have I, Tom? Never tried to convert you? It isn't the atheist way. We don't go out on missions or go door-to-door with pamphlets."

Charlie's laughter pealed out through the vastness as she spun around, her red hair vivid as a thrown splash of paint. "As my own mother would have said, Tom, your uncle is a caution."

Though I didn't know that particular way of putting it, I had long known that my uncle was unlike other men. Our province is still a very conservative place, and to be an atheist, an art lover, and an unapologetic critic of hockey, rodeos, and country music already placed him in a small minority, at least amongst men of his generation. Add to that his struggles with mental health, his tendency to associate with people of all ages and ethnicities, and his habit of keeping his hair and beard very long, and you had a man that would put many conservative people on their guard. Only his ownership of a truck and his wealth – he had been a GP for thirty years and had apparently made wise investments – seemed even remotely acceptable. As I was only twenty, my uncle provided me with a valuable and accessible means of testing how I felt about various aspects of life without putting myself at much risk. One thing was clear: there was no doubting his love for me. And in such an uncertain time, when everyone seemed so worried and

I had nothing but a desire to break out of all family and professional and religious restrictions, my uncle's love and his good spirit kept my faith in a different sort of future vitally alive.

That same evening, Uncle Francis and Charlie showed me the large industrial freezer where the roadkill was kept. Against the wall, next to Charlie's easels, stacked canvases and old frames, paints and turpentines, the big white rectangle hummed away under the fluorescent lighting like some sort of animal itself. From inside it, my uncle, with Charlie's permission, pulled out about a dozen specimens: a magpie, a porcupine, a skunk, and, largest of all, a coyote – whose fixed snarl seemed unnervingly on the point of life.

"Anything bigger," Francis explained, "has to go somewhere else. But fortunately, we haven't come upon a deer lately, never mind a bear or a moose."

"It's ironic," Charlie added. "In some ways, if we found more of the larger animals on the highway, it would be a good sign. It would mean that there were more of them still around."

"She doesn't regard one animal as more beautiful and important anyway." My uncle's shaggy bear-like face was beaming again. "She puts all of her talent into painting even a mouse."

"There's so much wonderful detail in a mouse though." Charlie stared off into some horizon that I figured only an artist could see. "But it isn't hard to find one to draw from life." Her voice dropped. "Or, that is, from death."

My uncle turned a suddenly horrified look on me. "But we're not hoping to find a bear or a moose. No, no, Tommy. It isn't like that. Collisions of that sort..."

"The only thing worse than roadkill," Charlie said, "is roadkill that brings emergency vehicles."

The words hung ominously in the hollow air, lightened only by the humming of the freezer. Then I helped my uncle carefully place the frozen corpses back inside.

"You can learn a lot from Charlie," he said, turning away from shutting the lid of the freezer. "About art. I've told her, you know. About your talent. She's not surprised. Says she could sense you weren't just being polite on these outings. If you're comfortable with it, she'd like to see some of your drawings. I told her I'd mention it to you."

The idea was exciting and unsettling at the same time. No one except my uncle had ever seen my drawings, and that had been several years before when I'd accidentally left a few of them on top of some of my math homework. After taking a deep breath, I said that maybe one day I'd bring something to show her.

Looking back now, I can't help but believe that my unusual pandemic life with Uncle Francis and Charlie would have carried on, if not for my father's intervention. He called me into his study one night after my uncle had dropped me off at home, and I could see disappointment all over his soft-featured thin face.

"You've not been telling me the truth, Tom," he said.

Before I could defend myself, he put his hand up.

"I know you have a special relationship with Francis. I respect that. But you're not helping him if you don't tell me how he is. More to the point, what he's doing and . . . who he's doing it with."

"He seems fine. He's not manic or anything. And he says he's taking his medication."

Never a man to waste time, my father cut to the point.

"We know about his female friend, Tom. That she's some sort of artist. Well, that's not the first of those he's been involved with over the years."

The way my father spoke of artists was much the way he'd speak of roadkill. Not with disgust, but certainly not with any respect either. For that reason, I'd always kept my own drawings a secret.

"And the fact of the matter is, Francis is an elderly man and an independent one, and I can have no influence with him on anything." My father stood up from behind his desk and looked straight at me with an unsettling intensity that I knew well, even if it hardened his features only on rare occasions. "But you're my son, and I'd prefer you not to be a party to your uncle's sins."

"Sins?"

"His friend is married. Your mother and I don't want to condone that sort of relationship. And we'd like to believe, Tom, that you don't want to either. Now, I'm not saying that you shouldn't keep seeing your uncle. After all, I was the one who encouraged you to see more of him. But it would be best if you saw him when he's on his own."

Everything in my father's voice and attitude suddenly made me angry. But he wasn't a man I'd ever been able to stand up to. After all, I'd kept playing hockey and going to church mostly because I'd lacked the courage to disappoint him. Now, however, perhaps the strangeness of the world and my sudden closeness to my uncle made me brave.

"Charlie's very nice," I said, swallowing hard. "And I think Uncle Francis loves her. I don't... I don't think there's anything sinful about it."

My father, typically, seemed neither surprised nor unsurprised by my words. In fact, he didn't appear to give them serious consideration.

"Sin isn't something you know very much about," he said, and smiled as if he was explaining a drill at hockey practice. "Because you've been raised properly."

The smile, more than his tone, made the muscles in my whole body tighten. Yet I could barely find the breath to say what I couldn't hold back. "Wasn't Uncle Francis raised properly, then?"

"Your uncle," my father said with more hostility than sadness, "has made bad choices. But then, as you know, he isn't a well man."

What is a well man? I wanted to ask, knowing that the answer would only clarify what I already understood to be the growing problem between us. So I just nodded, feeling somehow disloyal to my uncle and Charlie.

As it turned out, my protestations wouldn't have mattered, because Uncle Francis, who had learned of the family's objections, conceded to my parents' wishes. "There's no sense in upsetting them on the matter," he explained. "Not while you're living with them. It's one thing for me to be the black sheep, but you're just getting your wool."

Despite the sadness in his voice, his blue eyes twinkled over his dirty white shag of beard. "Not to worry. One day, I'll make an honest woman of Charlie. More to the point, she'll make an almost honest man of me. Then we can come over to dinner once you get your first apartment."

. . .

A WEEK LATER, my uncle's truck was hit head-on by a pandemic-crazed joyrider speeding in the wrong direction. Charlie was pronounced dead at the scene, and Francis was rushed in critical condition to the nearest hospital that could accommodate him amongst the swelling numbers of Covid victims. Fully masked, we were only allowed in to see him two people at a time.

I'd never had any experience of hospitals, and so entering one during a pandemic was especially eye-opening and alarming. Of course, I was already numb with grief for Charlie and terrified that I would also lose Francis, but even in that state I could recognise that the chaos was unusual, as well as the extreme caution. The workers were fully clad in what looked like outer space gear (full plexiglass shields and those white bodysuits and tight yellow gloves) and most of the patients – in rooms and on portable beds in the hallways – were so hooked up to various tubes and IV bags and monitors that it was hard to even see them as human. And there were also a lot of upset patients and family members in and around the emergency room, waiting under the harsh glare of the fluorescent lights. Waiting for hours and hours. I could see the panic in their eyes above their masks.

But Uncle Francis wasn't suffering from Covid. His situation was already life-threatening enough. In fact, when my father and I were finally allowed to see him, in a room separate from the general and just-controlled chaos, it soon became clear that he wasn't expected to survive. A doctor told us, though, that he was conscious and showed signs of understanding. So I waited for my father to withdraw – he had the decency to understand I needed to be alone with my uncle for a while – and gently took Francis's large prominently-veined hand.

Though he had been sedated and needed a ventilator to help him breathe, he managed to mouth my name. I could see that the attempt at speech cost him a terrible effort, and as I already knew what was on his mind, I rapidly considered my choices.

"Charlie's fine," I said, fighting back tears. "She's going to be fine."

I thought, if he survives, he can face the loss of her when he's recovered; if he dies, it will do no good for him to know the truth beforehand. Believing she's alive might even give him the strength he needed to come through. Besides, I reassured myself, it wasn't exactly a lie. She was a good person, and that meant she was with God, if there was a God. What could be finer than that?

I felt a pressure on my hand, a surprising pressure. My uncle's lips fluttered rapidly.

"No..." he said. "No..."

He couldn't get the next words out, so I stood and leaned over his face. Beneath the clear plastic mask, his eyes were full of a haunted pleading I'd never seen. The terrible staccato beeping of machines came from near and far. I waited for what seemed like hours.

"Priest," he finally gasped, and widened his eyes. "Don't... let..."

It must have been my imagination, but I suddenly sensed my father's shadow falling over the bed.

"... them... no priest..."

Then his hand weakened and his eyes closed. The room shrank to the size of his face, and the walls, floor and ceiling fell away. All at once I was floating through space and intensely focused at the same time. I sensed what was coming, or, rather, what my uncle had asked of me, but I didn't know if I had the courage to protect his wishes. I did know, however, that I wouldn't have much time to choose. Already Francis seemed more than halfway out of his life.

As it turned out, only hours passed – in which the same doctor told us to be prepared for the worst – before the priest came through the automatic doors into the emergency room waiting area. I recognised him right away, of course, despite his mask, for I had known him all my life. Father Dougherty was elderly (it was well known that if you had a young priest, he wouldn't be European, but rather Mexican or South American – my uncle said that the Church had lost much of its hold over the western young) and well over six feet tall. I had always been alarmed by his height, but even more so by the remarkable length and whiteness of his neck. It always made me imagine that he'd been hanged for days without dying. For obvious reasons, priests generally have an aura of death around them, but Father Dougherty was particularly grim. It didn't help that his voice was gravelly and his speech excruciatingly slow. The pale blue mask only made him look even more like an executioner.

He and my father quickly began to conspire. At least that was how I saw it. There wasn't any more time left. I got up quickly and, ignoring the cries of a nurse, almost sprinted to my uncle's room. Positioning myself outside the door, I waited, trying to calm my pulse and my breathing.

As my father and the priest approached, their steps fell thunderously on my ears. The beeping of the machines might have been for me. I closed my hand and felt the terrible coldness of my uncle's there, a coldness that was soon to be glacial. The feeling should have made the idea of Hell easier to take, but it didn't. Not at all. Right up to the second that I physically blocked the priest from entering the room, every ounce of my being was telling me that I had no right to do this, because perhaps even my uncle had no right either. Who were we to stand up to centuries of belief? Yet I could act because I didn't feel that I was doing it for myself, even if, at some deep level, I was.

I could sense but not see the old priest's familiar slow smile.

"Hello, Thomas. I'm truly sorry for what has happened. A terrible, terrible thing." It took ages for him to get these words out, long enough for my father to appear beside me.

"Let Father Dougherty by, Tom. I know you're upset, but there isn't time for any foolishness. Your uncle needs to be at peace with God."

I managed only to shake my head, knowing that my voice would be weak if I spoke again. My whole body was cold.

"Tom."

My father put his hand on my shoulder and gently pushed. I didn't move.

Now the tall, masked priest lingered to the side exactly like an executioner waiting as the final preparations for the axe-blow are made.

"He doesn't want him," I said. "He's an atheist. You know he is."

My father turned to the priest. Because they both wore masks, their eyes seemed more violent in their expressiveness. My father turned back.

"Your uncle wants to be with God. And with his family too, Tom. With his parents. That's what he wants. He doesn't want to be lost. Alone. Suffering."

"You don't know him like I do. He told me. He made it very clear." I looked hard at Father Dougherty. "No priest."

My father sighed. "I know him better than you think. More to the point, God knows him. This is too important, Tom, for you to get involved with. Move aside and let

Father Dougherty past. Your uncle's soul is at stake here. Stop being foolish. You're old enough to know better."

But I wasn't old enough, that was the point. If I had been, I wouldn't have trembled so much from fear and doubt.

"A man such as your uncle," Father Dougherty said, his words as stark and separate as the beeps of the machines, "a good man. He would come back to God now. If not for himself, then for his family. That is what he would do."

The beeping intensified and seemed to push at my back. Suddenly nurses and doctors, who had been in constant motion in the general area around us, were flitting about like trapped bats.

"Tom!"

When my father grabbed me by both shoulders and pulled, I didn't hesitate. I reached out and, with all my strength, threw him to the floor. Then I widened my stance across the doorway, planting my legs as firmly as tree trunks into the earth. Flashing lights appeared near the ceiling all along the hallway, like a lit fuse leading right up to the hem of the priest's black robe.

"It is a grave decision you are making, son," Father Dougherty said, and his voice echoed all around me. "And one you will come to regret. It is much, much worse than doing violence to your own father." He took a step towards me. "Or to a servant of God."

I put my trembling hand up. I might even have made a fist.

"Assaulting God," he said, "is damnation. And damnation's more terrible than you can imagine."

But I wouldn't move, except to let the nurses and doctors by.

My father lunged at my right shoulder, but I knocked his arm away and raised my clenched fist towards him. "If I have to, I'll throw you down again." My voice and my body trembled so much that I wasn't sure I could stay upright, let alone do what I threatened.

"You ungrateful little shit," my father said, his face twisted and red, as if he was attacking a referee between periods. "What the hell do you think you're playing at? Get the fuck out of the way before I..."

Father Dougherty put his pale, long-fingered hand on my father's chest. Then he calmly began to detail the eternal torment and horrible loneliness into which I was sending my beloved uncle. But I could hardly take the words in. Every ounce of me was tensed for a physical attack. In fact, the more my father and the priest challenged me, the more my resolve deepened. The whole time – and this was the hardest thing – I was half-convinced to relent, but something kept me on the path I had chosen. It was too late to change course.

I knew, without even thinking about them, that the consequences of my actions would be significant. I knew that nothing else I did would ever cause my family any greater pain, not even if I died myself. I knew that I was choosing my own life to be my uncle's afterlife.

Somehow the tense ordeal ended. A doctor spoke to us and said that Francis was gone. But still I would not move aside to let my father and the priest into the room. I didn't trust them. In truth, I didn't know the exact procedures of a Catholic death. Perhaps there was a grace period after the heart stops beating when the last rites can still be given. I couldn't take the chance.

All my father's habitual pretend kindness had long since drained out of him. Ignoring the priest's presence again, he said, "You goddamned selfish little bastard. If you think that your uncle's money means that you can turn your back on your family, then I'll do everything I can to contest his will. I'll prove that he wasn't in his right mind. I'll hire the best lawyer in town. No child of mine is going to make a fool of himself if I can help it."

"Make a fool of you, you mean." I still held my forearms straight up in front of me, prepared to move quickly. My father's reference to my likely inheritance, shocking as the information was, only strengthened my resolve. I didn't know how he knew about my uncle's will – maybe Francis had told him, in an unguarded moment or even as a sort of taunt. It made no difference, of course. No matter what he said, my father and the priest weren't getting into the room.

After another few minutes, which felt like hours, the threats and the swearing stopped. All at once, my father and the priest were gone. The hallway seemed darker, even if it wasn't. And the beeping of the machines came from a greater and greater distance away. Without God, my uncle, at the end, needed someone.

So I stayed with his corpse until I was told that I couldn't stay any longer. I stayed as the darkness closed all around me and I heard the great rushing sounds of coming death. I thought then of what Charlie had once said about animals, why she loved them enough to go out on the highways and gather their broken bodies and preserve and mourn them with her talent. "It is because they are always exactly themselves," she had said. "They are true to their own natures, even if the truth will often kill them."

Already I sensed that I waited to cross the same darkness, but my body was no longer shaking, and my mind was beginning to clear as I walked out of the hospital into the roaring hush of the strange and new world, made even stranger and newer by my deeper loneliness inside it.

The Librarian's Dilemma

. . .

— I —

SHE WAS the first girl Adam had ever kissed – poorly, not quite meeting her mouth, and she had smiled gently afterwards, pushing her hair from her eyes as if trying to move a spiderweb without harming the spider – and he was determined not to lose her attention. The threat came from an older boy, a newcomer to town, with long black hair, blue eyes, and a body as lean as Christ's on the cross, the white skin showing like epaulettes here and there through the coppery tan. He had arrived only a few weeks before, in mid-summer, on a catamaran, an ungainly-looking craft. Adam found it hard to believe that Ray, along with his parents and sister, had actually sailed around the world in something that resembled a giant water bug. Besides, if they had sailed around the world, why would they choose to stop in a small town on the Fraser River that smelled of rotting salmon and rotting cabbages most of the time?

On the gravel dyke above the river, Adam raised the question now, but without mentioning the salmon and cabbages, and watched carefully for Jackie's reaction.

Ray bounced a small rock on the palm of one hand, then whipped it at the cannery roof, scattering a flock of dirty seagulls.

"Got to stop somewhere. And Lisa wanted us to go to proper school for a change."

Jackie's smile was slight and hard to read. Her upper lip was swollen on account of a bee sting, but Adam somehow knew she was impressed with the answer. Who else ever called his mother by her first name? If Adam had ever called *his* mother by her first name, the wooden spoon would have come straight out of the drawer. He suddenly felt stupid, like a little boy. Even the bulge of fat at the top of his cut-off jeans was babyish compared to Ray's hard brown flesh in which the ribs showed clearly. And yet Adam had kissed Jackie only a few nights before; the smell of her skin – part grape bubble-gum, part grass, part something he couldn't begin to describe – hovered around him still.

The gulls settled on the sloped roof again. Every few seconds one screeched and opened its wings and beak wide. Adam looked to the west where more gulls appeared, flying in from the ocean, headed towards the garbage dump up the river. He tried to stop himself, but he couldn't help it; Jackie's warm brown eyes watched Ray's every move.

"If your mom wants you to go to proper school, why doesn't she make you call her by her proper name?"

Ray narrowed his eyes, then smirked. "That is her name, stupid. Do you think I should call her Mommy like you probably call yours?"

Jackie laughed. She was twelve, the same age as Ray; they were both starting high school the next week. Desperately, Adam watched her shadow in the dusk edge away from him. He swallowed drily; his legs felt weak. He had lived next-door to Jackie for five years; it wasn't fair that some other kid could just sail into the neighbourhood and replace him so easily in her affections. Over the pounding of his blood, he could barely hear himself speak, but he knew his lips were moving.

"Everybody calls their mom mom."

"Mom mom? Have you got two of them, then?" Ray's voice had a slight accent. He bragged that he'd picked it up in Australia.

Jackie's white teeth flashed under her swollen lip. Her long brown hair swung over her bare shoulder as she leaped onto the log beside Ray.

Adam struggled to stop but it was impossible. "No. But at least I've got a real dad. Not just my mom's boyfriend."

Ray jumped on him almost before the last word had left Adam's mouth. In seconds, there was the taste of blood where there had been the taste of Jackie's skin. He lay face down in the sharp gravel, Ray's knee in his back.

"Who told you that, you fat fuck? Huh? Huh?"

The knee pressed harder. Pain flared across Adam's left cheek. Out of his right eye he could see only a green and black blur of blackberry bush beyond Jackie's motionless figure.

"Let him go," she said, her voice not concerned or frightened, just bored.

Ray lifted his knee, dropped it hard once into the small of Adam's back, then stood. For a while only Ray's quick breathing and Adam's sniffling efforts to fight back tears disturbed the quiet. Then the breathing was gone, and the two shadows on the gravel also. Adam swallowed and swallowed, trying to recover that taste of gum and grass and the thing he couldn't name. But only the slightly metallic taste of his blood came to his tongue.

Finally, he rolled over and pulled himself into a sitting position. In the distance, down the slope of the dyke and across the vacant lot of waist-high grass and wild, untended cherry trees, he saw Ray and Jackie walking towards town. They weren't close enough together to be holding hands, but it didn't matter. Adam knew that if he didn't do something soon, they'd be closer than handholding and he'd never be able to separate them. He watched their bodies diminish as he stood and wiped blood into the tears that had rolled down his cheek. From far off came the harsh barking of a dog. Second by second, it came closer, until finally it seemed to originate under Adam's own heartbeat, stray, never tamed, the sound of the response he knew he would have to make if he wanted to recover what he had just begun to lose.

— II —

I LIKE TO stay late, after the library closes. Alone in the stacks, I can experience for a brief time that curious sensation of faith in humankind's intelligence, compassion, and poetry that only an accumulation of books can arouse. Some librarians – in fact, the majority in the small towns where I've worked over the past fifteen years – at least pretend to enjoy the interaction with the public that the job involves. Not me. I make no bones about preferring books to people. After all, I've never known a book to jump up and tear a piece of skin off a human face or to write something lewd and ignorant across a forehead. The abuse that the innocent book undergoes! Some days I have to grit my teeth when doing my job, and once I've worn them down to the nub, I seek a transfer to another branch, just to vary the people. Circulation isn't only a matter of what a town reads, but also of what a librarian can endure. And as I've said, my endurance lasts only so long.

The kid just appeared one day, bold as brass, shirtless, barefoot, and immediately set about flipping through a comic. I told him he had to be dressed properly to use the library. He sneered at me from under a head of long curls that resembled shavings of black soap. His full mouth had the same insolent, greasy curve to it. I disliked him straight off. For me, children and adults are exactly the same; some you like, some you don't. There's an instinct involved. And mine's tuned finer than a Steinway.

After the sneer, the kid said, "I just finished anyway," and tossed the comic on a table.

I winced at the way the cover splayed. "How about closing it properly?"

"You're the one who works here," he said, and left.

I swallowed some spit – library schools ought to offer courses in that particular skill – and neatly placed the comic on its rack.

The next time the kid came in, he wasn't alone. He had a girl with him, a pretty girl too. Well, I was too old to be surprised by the idiot boy–pretty girl facts of life. It was sad, though. For the girl, yes. But more so for the chubby boy who seemed to be tagging along. I recognised him, of course. He was a regular, liked to read *Encyclopedia Brown* mysteries and Time-Life books on dinosaurs and insects, stuff like that. Pretty ordinary bookish sort of kid. Always wore a shirt and shoes in the library, even on the hottest days. My heart would have gone out to him, if my heart had had the energy. He tried so hard to get the girl's attention, showing her pictures in books. The little sap! I wanted to whisper in his ear, "Listen, girls like that aren't interested in the thorax of the red ant." But it was just the world going about its tawdry, embarrassing business; I tried not to pay attention.

However, the black-haired kid – surprise, surprise – was sniggering loudly over the big dictionary on the stand, impressing the girl with his remarkable capacity for looking up dirty words. A young Macbeth and Lady Macbeth, that's what I thought. And the chubby boy as innocent as one of Duncan's grooms about to be slaughtered.

I would have found something else to occupy me then, but the sniggering kid decided that dirty words weren't entertaining enough. So he made a big show of taking off his shirt. All right, I sighed, if that's how you want to play it.

"I told you already. No shirt, you can't be here."

"Yeah? I don't see any sign." He looked at the chubby boy and nodded. But the chubby boy just blushed and looked at his feet. The pretty girl did a wonderful impersonation of a pretty girl melting into the background as she stepped into the foreground, all without moving so much as a hair. I had known women like that. The knowledge kept me single.

"No sign," I said calmly. "Put your shirt back on or you'll have to leave."

"Yeah?" He snickered and pointed at the little name tag I had to wear on my shirt. "What if I don't want to, Pink?"

The girl caught her breath in a half giggle.

I sighed the sigh of Matthew Arnold at Dover Beach. When your name is Floyd, you get used to certain things from pubescents. And then, later, those pubescents sometimes become undergraduates inspired enough to call you Sigmund. The world's awash in such wit.

"Not original, Sonny boy. About as original as showing off by being a tough guy in a library."

The "Sonny boy" proved a hit, a most palpable hit. This kid was sensitive to even the tiniest insult. But I wasn't too concerned. I'm over six feet tall, broad across the shoulders, and my uneven teeth, when displayed to full effect, intimidate people a lot older than twelve or thirteen. More than a few women have told me that I look like a pirate. Floyd Jarvis, the Terror of the Barbary Main Branch, that's me. So, it was a surprise when the kid spat on the floor, gave me the finger, and returned to flipping through the dictionary.

I didn't even think about it first, just pounced, put him in a half nelson and frogmarched him out the door. The filth that poured out of his mouth brought the branch manager running from his office, and several old ladies emerged from around the carousels of paperback romances, the scowls on their faces making little dagger swipes at the kid's face.

Of course I wasn't proud of myself. Normally I'm a paragon of self-control, but I was getting close to seeking a transfer; the kid just picked the wrong time to spread his peacock feathers for his peahen.

Once we got outside, I hurled him away from me, but he turned immediately, snarling like a cornered cougar. Spit sprayed from his mouth as he called me every current dirty name and even a few from the glorious Anglo-Saxon tradition. Obviously this pretty girl wasn't the first to witness his lexicographical prowess in a public library. I glanced at her out of the corner of my eye. She and the chubby boy stood, almost touching, wide-eyed; they might have been brother and sister at a circus, watching the lion-tamer act. But I had no interest in performing for them. I had to go back inside and justify my actions to my superior, who was in most ways my inferior, but I've already mentioned the tawdry, embarrassing business of the world.

Then the kid dropped his bombshell.

"I'll torch the fuckin' place!" he shouted and made a histrionic display of what appeared to be emptying a gasoline can and tossing a lit match into it. Either that or he was simulating masturbation. But I suppose violence and sex amount to the same thing at that age; I don't really remember. In any case, my presence was just like gasoline on the kid's rage, so I deployed all the wisdom of my forty years and retreated to the relative calm of the Dewey Decimal System.

For a couple of minutes the kid's shouts continued. I had the strange sensation that a goldfish must experience when a dog barks up against its bowl. My superior, after instructing me to never, ever use physical force on a patron, phoned the cops. But of course the kid vanished long before the constabulary appeared. Probably he had already started the process of ditching the chubby boy so he could get his hands down the pretty girl's pants. I had more important things to think about. There were postings in Merritt and Prince Rupert, the dry and the wet, cowboys and fishermen and, without a doubt, more idiot boys and pretty girls. The world keeps turning no matter where an itinerant librarian puts his feet.

— III —

THE CHERRIES HAD never been so plentiful. In backyards and vacant lots all over town, the eyeball-sized, almost black fruit hung so thick from the branches that not even the starlings and robins made much of an impression in the supply. High up in a tree near the dyke, Adam had not moved in nearly an hour; he just kept reaching his hand out every minute and finding a perfect specimen. His lips were stained purple. Beyond him, the heavy August sun was a giant cherry splitting apart with its own ripeness and staining the horizon. The gulls on the cannery roof shrieked in a fury of appetite.

Adam spat out another pit. That made forty-three. At the same pace, once he'd reached seventy, it would be dark and he could climb down, gather his supplies from where he'd stashed them in the reeds by the government wharf. His hand trembled; once he almost fell off his perch. The cherries were warm as blood in his mouth. But it was a good taste, not shameful like the taste of his own blood had been. He waited until the darkness came softly down over him, smelling of summer and skin, of the time before Ray, the time he was determined to get back.

Fifteen minutes later, crouched, progressing like a wounded bat, he hurried out of the park and attached himself to the rear of the library. His breath flowed ragged, fast as his heartbeats. He would not allow himself to be afraid. The air was full of the smell of her kiss; it permeated even the sickly-sweet fumes rising from the gas can he'd taken from his father's shed. But the kiss would be even stronger once the fumes were gone. Rapidly he emptied the can, the gas splashing and then spurting; some spilled on his pant leg. He dropped the can and fumbled with the box of wooden matches; it took four strikes before the tiny light blazed up and he flicked it from him as if his fingers burned. The whoosh of flame shocked him. He jumped back, started to run, almost collided with a parked car whose black shape in the dark he discovered just in time.

The fire took hold fast. It had been dry and hot for weeks and the wood of the library crackled fiercely. In minutes an orange giant was pressed against the building, crunching on bones. Adam caught his breath against the knotted trunk of an old pear tree, then noticed he'd forgotten the most important thing. Briefly, he struggled to find the courage to run back. Jackie's face flashed into his mind, the way she moved the hair from her eyes. He clenched the T-shirt in his hand; it seemed to laugh, dangling from his hand like Ray's severed head. Adam sprang forward. When he was close enough to suit his purpose, he dropped the shirt. Just then, lights flicked on inside the library. Adam felt a thousand eyes on him, the crouching giant turned greedily in his direction. This time, when he fled, he did not stop until the sirens had begun to scream at his back and he was shaking and panting in the cherry tree by the dyke, the fruit so black around him it might have been scorched.

— IV —

IF I HADN'T fallen asleep over a copy of the Fraser Valley Library Bulletin (you try staying awake; I offer a fiver to all comers), the whole place would have burnt to a crisp and probably me along with it. As it was, we lost a few hundred books, mostly juveniles, appropriately enough since I knew that a juvenile had committed the deed. One of life's little ironies, as Thomas Hardy would say.

A fireman brought the shirt in. White and yellow with a grinning kangaroo on it. Well, well, I thought. The night should have been astir with sparrows attacking owls and other spooky Shakespearean portents. The kid had certainly screwed his courage to the sticking place. When I gave the shirt to the cops, of course I had to answer their questions. Had I ever seen it before? Yes. Did I remember who wore it? Yes. Had that person ever threatened to burn down the library? Ok, the cops didn't exactly ask that one right away, but they got around to it on account of the incident only two days before, which the branch manager was more than happy enough to delineate for them. Pretty damning evidence. And it can never be too damning for the authorities when a smartass kid with hippie parents, one of whom turns out to be only the mother's boyfriend, a dope-smoking captain of the family catamaran, of all things, is implicated.

The question was, the question is, how damning was it for me? I spent a bad night before the cops called me down to the station and put me in a room with all three kids. I sat at a table across from them and some government agent for juveniles and felt like Banquo at the feast, except it was a hell of a lot easier for him; Macbeth wasn't just some messed-up kid when he slipped old Duncan the blade.

The pretty girl hadn't cracked as badly as Macbeth's good lady. At least, she wasn't scrubbing spots of fire off her hands. She was deeply tear-stained, however, and very badly frightened. And completely innocent too, certainly in the strictest legal terms. I assumed she'd been brought in, along with the chubby boy, because the three of them were so often seen together.

The black-haired kid was much calmer than I'd expected. "You're a fuckin' liar," he said to me, not loud or violent, almost matter-of-fact, though his hands trembled and he kept picking at the chipped paint on the tabletop. The agent – a prim woman in a bright pantsuit – whispered in his ear and he scowled. "I told you already, it wasn't me. It was . . . "

The room became a huge held breath. The fluorescent lights hummed a little. But the black-haired kid just looked at the pretty girl and clammed up.

"Who? Who was it, then?" a large cop said with obvious scepticism. T-shirt, threat, fire, hippie household – or boat-hold or whatever you want to call it: he knew what guilty looked, smelled, and walked like.

And me? Listen, I'm a librarian but that doesn't make life any easier. Books can broaden and deepen your experience on this blue planet, but they don't have all the answers. I know that much. Besides, I'm an indifferent librarian, a drifter, unmarried, father to nothing but my precious misanthropy which I keep leashed like an exotic pet. Left to myself, I'd just keep drifting, job to job, town to town, book to book, fresh air to the grave. But as I sat there in that station, with the embryonic and the autocratic and the bureaucratic representatives of the human condition gathered around me, I couldn't feed the pet on the leash and I couldn't let it go. The chubby boy's eyes never left my face. I blinked at him. He seemed to lean forward, as if he wanted a hug, as if he was the kid I never had or even wanted to have. What the hell was I doing in such a spot? A father should have to make such a call, or at least an uncle or a friend of the family. I wasn't anything to anyone. And yet the kid leaned forward. I couldn't not meet his eyes. They didn't help. Because he was ordinary, normal, a boy who'd never have a chance with a pretty girl until he was a lot older and the pretty girls were pretty women tired of idiot boys and pirate-librarians and wanting something he could offer. And just to set the record straight, I didn't dislike the black-haired kid because I'd once been like him. Listen to me! Life isn't that simple. I was never the chubby boy or the punk. I was... well, what were you? I was myself. And now I was that same self but thirty years older and all the silent gods of the human condition were waiting for an answer.

I began to sweat. The aisles of all the libraries I'd ever worked in appeared and pressed around me. Christ! I wasn't Macbeth. Fatal visions weren't my line at all.

The cops shifted their beefy weight. The pantsuited woman sighed and snapped her briefcase shut. The black-haired kid stared down the simmering violence of all the years ahead of him and nothing I said was going to stop that cold sight. His lip curled like a caterpillar tossed in a fire. I looked away. The problem wasn't even that I had to live with myself. What else had I been doing for years, too many years to count? Lillooet, White Rock, North Vancouver, Prince George. It was always the same. The world turned and would keep turning. And the girl and the fat boy and maybe even the punk would grow up and become citizens. Citizens! The animal strained at the leash.

I cleared my throat.

"He did it," I said, and pointed. "I saw him. Plain as day. I saw him running across the parking lot. It was him."

There was noise, a response of some kind, motion. I was washed clear of it somehow, clear of the papers and the signings and the scowls, until I found myself outside, walking down a silent street in Pernod sunlight. Starlings were attacking a cherry tree in someone's yard. The owner of the tree had hung tinfoil pie plates on the branches to scare the birds, but the ploy didn't work. The starlings tore the flesh of the tree to shreds. The sun flashed on the pie plates and the black wings of the birds darkened the branches as if night had already fallen. I watched for a few minutes, the leash slackening, before I returned to the overdues and the card catalogues and the never-ending circulation of the ordinary life.

The Boat Ride

. . .

MY FATHER, gumbooted and skullcapped, with a switched-off flashlight in hand, stood on the braided mat by the kitchen door, speaking softly to my mother. She wore her housecoat and slippers, so I knew without even looking at the clock that it was very late.

"What's happened?" I said, surveying all the chair-backs for my coat, just in case.

My mother sighed. "Go back to bed, Nate. There isn't any fishing."

I already knew there wasn't any fishing because I knew the scheduled openings better than anyone. Once school ended in June, and before it started again in September, I phoned the Department of Fisheries and Oceans' recorded message three or four times a day. Even now, a month and a half into another school year, with dew heavy on the spider-webs and on the pumpkins as orange as salmon roe in the fields, I phoned the DFO just to hear the list of zones that had closed – Bella Coola, Bamfield, Ucluelet. The names were a sort of lullaby to the seasons I already sensed I would miss as much as I would miss my father himself one day.

Headlight beams poured through the window and slid along the wall above my parents' heads. When the beams clicked off, my parents seemed to inhabit a greater darkness than they had just a few seconds before. An engine shut off and a car door closed. There was a crunching sound as someone walked up our crushed gravel driveway.

"Who's that?" I turned from one parent to the other. "What's going on?"

"It's Dr. Kaney," my mother said, clutching the two sides of her nightgown together at her neck. "I wonder if I should put the kettle back on. He might like a tea before you go." She looked at my father, who shook his head.

"He's a busy man. Look what time it is now."

He wasn't speaking to me, but I raised my eyes to the clock on the wall anyway. 1:17.

The doctor's footsteps clumped on the wooden stairs, and I didn't hesitate. I hurried into my room and pulled on a pair of jeans. Then, back in the kitchen, just after the door opened and the doctor's shadow fell on the braided mat, I discreetly found my coat and pulled it on. It didn't much matter to me why my father and Dr. Kaney were going out together in the early hours of the October morning, but since they obviously were, I knew that the outing involved our boat and the river.

"Good evening. How's the young scholar today?"

Dr. Kaney's slight smile seemed broad due to the fullness of his lips and to his general grave demeanour. A heavy-set man with remarkably bulbous eyes and a permanent five o'clock shadow, he always reminded me of a slightly down-on-his-luck Alfred Hitchcock. Because he spoke more slowly than anyone else I knew, and because he was connected in my mind primarily with illness and boredom (the wait to be called into his office during my infrequent visits was always interminable), I both respected and feared him. The adults in my life were not professionals; in fact, most, including my parents, had not completed high school. The college certificates on the walls of Dr. Kaney's office might as well have been hieroglyphics.

But because he spoke to me as I put on my coat and made a passing reference to my recent honours status in grade eight, my parents must have interpreted his words as an invitation. Whatever the case, no one objected as I hurriedly pulled on my boots.

"I apologise for the hour," the doctor said, "but I had a delivery tonight and early rounds at the hospital in the morning."

"I'm a night owl anyway," my father said. "I'd just be poking a stick into a fire in the yard."

"Mrs. Maxwell is very concerned." The doctor's eyelids slid halfway over his bulging eyeballs before sliding back again. Even on waking, he must have always looked exhausted. "Otherwise, I would not think to ask for your help at such an ungodly hour."

My mother, handing a brown paper bag to my father, said, "There have been many times when you've come to us in the middle of the night. When Cindy had rheumatic fever."

Again, the slow smile that did not part the lips, and a kind of half bow. "I remember. A fever of 105. I was impressed that you had not called me sooner."

My parents, children of the Great Depression who had married during wartime, had an exaggerated respect for authority, especially medical authority, and an individual capacity not to trouble it unless absolutely necessary.

"Be sure you have some sandwiches and tea," my mother said as the men turned to the door. "I made plenty. Harold, there's the basket too."

"Nate can grab that."

As I bent to pick it up, Dr. Kaney said, "Provisions will be more welcome than us, I'm afraid."

My parents looked quickly at each other, a glance I understood to mean, "Helen Maxwell doesn't exaggerate"; it also meant, "Nate would not be going if there was any real danger"; finally, it meant what I had by now grasped: we were going to Alf Harley's island.

Dr. Kaney tightened the belt of his beige trench coat across his ample stomach. His five o'clock shadow seemed an inch thicker than when he'd arrived, his jowls a little more pronounced, as if pulling the belt triggered physical changes on his face. "Shall we?" He placed his hand, hairy as a werewolf's paw, on the doorknob and, nodding good evening to my mother, opened the door and walked out. My father and I followed.

In the narrow side yard stood a large Gravenstein apple tree. The thick aroma of its last windfall rose from the wet grass but wasn't strong enough to mask the smell of the river for long. As if the dyke had burst, the river pushed its tide of mud, brine, dead fish, and leaf mulch across our low-lying little town of potholed streets, straw-filled dog houses, and backyard gardens now in their tattered harlequin stage. The tide seemed to swing the dead pheasants hanging on the black branches of the apple tree, their beaks pointing downward, still dripping blood because my older brother had hung the catch there only a few hours before, just after dusk. The tide even seemed to make the faint stars shiver.

Beyond the tree, outside the jonquil shine of the porch light, the darkness possessed a material thickness, falling in alluvial folds off the sharp edge of the invisible moon. Once we'd left the driveway, we heard, more than saw, each other. Neither my father nor the doctor bothered with small talk, and I already knew that the questions I wanted to ask would be answered soon enough, so we completed the few minutes' walk to the government wharf in silence except for the doctor's harsh breathing. He was perhaps a decade older than my father, and considerably larger; we walked behind him as if tracking a wounded bear.

On the deck of my father's small gillnetter, a broad-sterned, shallow vessel designed to cope with the shifting sandbars and flowing muds and silts of the river mouth, Dr. Kaney lit a cigarette and gazed westward, downriver. I saw half of his rough, bouldery face in the match's flare and then, embarrassed by the silence throbbing above the coughing engine, I slipped into the cabin.

My father, at the wheel, held an unlit cigarette between his lips. It dangled expertly from the corner of his mouth as he peered into the dim spotlight beam for signs of floating logs or even just driftwood large enough to damage the propeller. The harbour channel was narrow, not more than two hundred feet from bank to bank, the town side cluttered with wharves, net sheds, moored boats of various sizes – from long aluminum herring skiffs to Jove-browed seiners – the river side just marsh grass broken intermittently by the charred candelabra of a weeping willow.

I stood beside my father, above the uncovered engine, mesmerised as always by the motion of the pistons and the fan belt, not quite sickened by the gas fumes. I wanted to shout a question above the steady noise, but somehow to do so seemed violent with the reserved doctor on board. So I just watched the wild bank of the mainland dissolve into the waving grassy point as my father, knowing the underwater layout of the sandbars, kept going when it seemed that he might turn upriver towards the north and the distant clump of ski lights on Grouse Mountain. Indeed, he almost touched the eastern bank of the first silt island before he turned the wheel and chugged along at a few knots past the graveyard of deadheads dragged into place by fishermen tired of snagging their nets on the same heavy hazards.

The tide was running out, I knew, because the deadheads all pointed downriver, like dogs straining at the leash, and we seemed to inch up the muddy bank even though the engine rattled and throbbed and I almost gagged on the fumes. Carefully, my father took his cigarette from his lips, and then, like a Japanese servant, bowed as he backed out of the cabin and assumed a safe smoking position at the deck-wheel.

For a moment, I thought we'd lost Dr. Kaney overboard. But to my surprise, he'd moved into the stern, behind the large wooden drum on which two hundred fathoms of net were wrapped, and was gazing back towards town, his hands behind his back. Somehow his two positions, the one leaning oceanward, the other landward, troubled me. It was as if, during our short journey, he'd made an important decision, and one that I couldn't understand. But at least he'd carried his black medical bag with him into the stern; whatever he'd decided, at least he hadn't given up medicine.

Within five minutes we had turned down one of the broad sloughs between the islands. A metre of mud showed between the river and the grass along each bank – occasionally the tide tore a chunk of mud off and it splashed soundlessly under the surface and the drone of our engine. I shuddered each time at the sight. Already the chill southeasterly wind had penetrated my clothing and my gloveless hands grew heavier by the second as the numbness set in. But I realised that the shuddering had a human source.

For one thing, it was strange to be out on the boat with no intention of setting a net. My father was not a recreational sort of man, and I was not old enough to be allowed to take the boat out on my own. For another thing, we never had non-family members on board. Finally, no one – and this was a fact that, at twelve, I could fathom only in the way that I could study a heron's shadow to understand flight – ever went near Alf Harley. Oh, you'd drift along his island, of course, and sometimes see the smoke rising from whatever grove of cottonwoods he'd dragged his boat into all those years ago, but you never saw the man. And, apparently, he never left the island either. My father, without regarding the situation as noteworthy in any way, described Alf Harley as a hermit. When I'd pressed him on the subject, during some lazy slack tide a few summers before, his answer had been brief and direct: "He doesn't like being around people, that's all. Prefers his own company."

"Doesn't he ever get lonely?"

"I guess not," my father finally said, gazing off along his cork line, and turning his back on Alf Harley's island.

"But what about his family? Doesn't he have any?"

"A sister, I think. Back in England. But I'm not sure."

And I knew there was no sense in pursuing the matter; I could tell from my father's tone that he had exhausted his store of information, or at least his willingness to share it.

I turned from studying the muddy bank to see Dr. Kaney's outline, just visible in the miniscule amount of mast-light, still frozen in place. Beyond him, like a dirty, underwater moon, the face of the town clock hovered, the hands unclear, the hour unknown. Even time seemed to feel the deepening frost that settled over and around us.

We left one slough and slipped into another, much narrower one, perhaps forty feet wide. At the mouth of the Fraser River, some sloughs act as channels between the half-dozen small islands, and some sloughs serve as entryways into the islands themselves. The latter are, naturally, more secretive, somehow shrouded without overhanging foliage to obscure them.

My father cut the engine and the night came alive. Or, rather, the silence deepened, even in its tricklings and creakings of current and tree limbs. Somehow, the river drew back like an arrow on a great black bow – all was tensile, quivering, and yet heavy with frost that seemed to come up from the island and down from the invisible stars. Back in the random groupings of cottonwoods and maples, their seedings a matter of river flow and wind direction, something appeared to be watching us, as if an owl perched on a pillar of Stonehenge gazed across the whole of England to see a small ship approaching the coast.

My father, pike pole in hand, tested the slough's depth as we drifted, slower and slower. Raising the long aluminum pole from the water and swinging it back down again, he resembled a tightrope walker. But if he fell, he would land in perhaps a dozen feet of silty water, which was alarming enough, for the current and the night air had the consistency of a La Brea tar pit. Great fossils with massive open jaws shifted and swirled like clouds on the river bottom and far above us. At any second, I could feel myself lifted or could see my father yanked down.

To gain my senses, I turned to the doctor. He had moved alongside the drum, onto the side-locker, half-crouched with the medical bag in his right hand, as if ready to leap overboard. For a moment, I stared at him, horrified, convinced that he would leap and vanish. I wanted to look away, but somehow my eyes were the stones and he was the pane of glass, and if I moved at all, there'd be a terrific smash and the river would bear his pieces away as easily as it shifted the tons of silt sifted down from the interior on every tide.

"This is about as far as we can go," my father said through a great spiderweb of breath. "Nate, see if you can tie us to a big stump or log."

He bent into the cabin and turned the spotlight on the bank. Rope in hand, I waited until a massive stump emerged out of the gloom, its roots as thick as my arm and tangled like a nest of snakes. The boat barely drifted now, so I had no trouble mooring us with a double hitch.

My father switched the spotlight off and the darkness dropped around us again. I could hear the doctor's laboured breathing as he moved up to the main deck, the tiny red glow of a cigarette in his free hand, which explained his breathing and his occasional harsh cough that now echoed like a gunshot over the island. Lonely or not, Alf Harley would almost certainly know by now that he had company.

The idea scared me even more when my father came out of the cabin with a lit, shimmering kerosene lamp in hand and announced that he would go on ahead to make sure . . .

of what he didn't specify, but I understood that Alf Harley, under normal conditions, discouraged company, and since these were not normal conditions, the other dangers had to be equally worrisome.

Using a root of the stump for leverage, my father easily hoisted himself over the bank, the light shaking around him like blossoms blown off a branch. Briefly, the island dark swallowed him as he crossed a low area, and then he reappeared, twenty seconds later – or rather his light did, fluttering erratically against the tree line like a big moth doused in phosphor.

Alone with the doctor, I immediately felt awkward. As I struggled to think of something to say, however, he surprised me by reading my mind.

"Everywhere's a kind of waiting room when you really think about it. But there aren't always magazines to look at. I think, for you, it might be a good idea to practise being alone with your own thoughts." He lifted the cigarette to his mouth, drew in, then broke into a shuddering cough that rang out across the watery island. "What I mean is . . ." I could almost hear the smile, slow as his blinking, take shape in the darkness. "There's no need to talk. I'm enjoying the quiet. I hope you don't mind."

Immensely relieved, I blurted out some kind of acceptance of his terms and retreated to the bow, where I sat cross-legged, my hand touching the cold, coiled anchor-chain. Alone with my thoughts, I tried, as a model student and as the son of parents who taught me to respect my elders, to practise *being alone with my thoughts*. But the self-consciousness of thinking about thinking – the kind of mental exercise that would define my mid-life years, mostly to their detriment – only made me more anxious for my father's reappearance. I tried to locate the Big and Little Dippers, or even the north star, but the night sky was too cloudy or too dark – and then I wondered if the night could in fact be so dark that the stars wouldn't show through. As soon as the thought occurred to me, my father's light, like a low star determined to disprove my theory, began to move towards the boat, or else the boat began to move towards my father's light. It was so quiet and so dark that all the normal time–space dimensions had ceased to operate. The night flowed tortuously towards dawn. An owl hooted somewhere in the vastness – two, three times – and I could almost hear the rapid panting and shivering of prey in the rushes and grasses.

I looked down into the slough and couldn't even tell its darkness apart from the night's. Desperately, I looked back up to see that my father's star had become a kerosene lantern and the outline of a man. I stood, my hand coming off the cold chain and immediately, briefly warming. By the time I'd reached the deck, both of my hands were chilled.

"There's no danger of being kept away," my father explained to Dr. Kaney. "He's in his bunk. Didn't respond when I spoke to him."

"Breathing?"

"Yes. But it doesn't sound right."

"But he's conscious?"

My father, standing three feet above us and bathed in light, possessed a frightening authority. Even so, he lowered his voice, perhaps for my sake, perhaps for the occasion's.

"I don't really know if you could call it that. But his eyes are open. When I held the light up, I could see that." My father shifted the lantern and vanished for a few seconds.

Then he added heavily, "But it didn't seem like he saw me even though he looked straight at me."

Dr. Kaney's cigarette slid through the dark air and sizzled when it hit the slough. He bent and picked up his black bag again. I could hear the instruments clink inside.

"Shall I take the light and go myself? You don't need to make the return trip."

My father's face turned thoughtful and even more serious. "I'd better. If he comes around, well, he'd recognise me."

Suddenly stricken at the thought of being left alone, even if I retreated into the cabin, I hurried to the stump and pulled myself onto the bank.

"I'm afraid I'm not such an athlete," the doctor said pleasantly. "You'll have to give me a hand, Harold."

A few minutes later, we started across Alf Harley's island. The ground was soft under the low grasses, muddy and silty, but not so soft we had to worry about losing our boots to the suction. My father guided us through the driftwood stumps and logs, avoiding the marshiest spots, walking slower than usual, probably on account of the doctor, whose heavy breathing was the only sound I heard as we crossed the island and came into the cottonwoods.

The six or seven trees seemed remarkably solid in the darkness – thick pillars of the air. Their few leaves shook ceaselessly, though, more like returning bats. I felt watched, and not with kindness. As a fisherman's son, I had no illusions about nature's relationship to the human world; in fact, part of the love and intimacy I knew for my surroundings depended on my knowledge of my meaningless fragility within them. And yet, I was scared now, and realised that I had been from almost the time we left the harbour. And what scared me most of all was that I sensed that the fear had a uniquely human source. Not the river or the night and its creatures posed any threat, but the doctor's solitary gazing from the stern, my father's body sinking and surfacing on the island, and, now, a gillnetter that had inexplicably been dragged into the trees and unevenly propped at the base of two trunks, its hull raised on our side as we approached, some kind of rough frame of drift lumber and rope holding the unusual habitation in place. The boat, about the size and shape of ours, had a cabin just as small, with little room sufficient for sleeping in. But what I saw I saw only in the wavering corona of light from my father's hand.

"Around here," he said to the doctor, and led the way past the stern to the port side where a large, levelled-off block of cedar provided a step up onto the deck. I wasn't asked to board, nor was I told to remain on the ground. Once my father and Dr. Kaney had boarded, I felt the eyes in the cottonwoods narrow; but much worse, I heard a voice far inside me that I'd never heard before, a voice telling me to stay where I was, alone. That choice, however, suddenly seemed no different than the other. The ground might just as easily have been deep water, but the boat, too, was made of water and offered no refuge. Finally, because I loved my father, I made the only choice I could and followed the shimmering light into the cabin.

The fetid smell almost knocked me back again. It seemed caked on the sloped interior sides of the hull in the bow where Alf Harley lay, a smell of sweat and vomit and urine and excrement. I clasped my hand to my mouth and nose and watched the giant, grotesque shadows of my father and the doctor swivel on the wood of the cramped space. Their shadows seemed to be feeding on the blanket-swaddled mass in the bunk.

The doctor's breathing slowly evened out. He opened his medical bag and removed a stethoscope and plunged it into the dark swaddling. His own material bulk slid together with his shadow and completely covered the upper half of the body in the bunk for several seconds. He asked my father to move the light closer. And the light seemed to flare up briefly, like a fire eating a gust of wind. Alf Harley's sunken eyes and unkempt beard drifted out of the gloom, then sank back under. The doctor said something in a low voice, either to himself, his patient, or my father. But there was no response. I hung where I had stopped, slightly above the three men, in the narrow space between the bunk and the wheelhouse. When the doctor rose, I half-expected to see blood dripping from his lips. But his face had remained the colour of his trench coat. This time, I heard what he said to my father, and the words also flared briefly before they turned irredeemably cold.

"He's dying."

"I figured as much," my father said after a weighty pause.

"We'll have to get him to town."

This time, the pause was longer and heavier. "When?"

Dr. Kaney's large eyes opened and closed, as if the lamplight had shed pollen on the lids. His voice was tired.

"As soon as possible. Now, if we can manage it."

"We can't." My father sounded relieved, though that didn't seem likely under the circumstances.

The doctor turned towards the bunk. "No, I don't imagine the three of us could manage. We'll have to come back. With reinforcements."

Immediately I saw eight fishermen, like pallbearers before the corpse was even a corpse, trudging across the island to the trees. And then, much worse, I saw them with their burden headed back the other way.

"How long has he got?" my father said.

"Not very. A few days, maybe a week. I'm surprised his heart has held up this long."

We all turned now, straining to hear the heartbeat through the thick flesh and heavy blankets.

"Can you give him something?" My father's voice did not soften, but I heard the tenderness in it.

The doctor stared at my father, as if his words were somehow more complex. Then he sighed. "To ease the pain, yes. But it would be better in the hospital. He'll be clean, and as comfortable as possible."

The river, the trees, the night all tensed behind me. I almost heard the words before the doctor spoke them.

"And he won't be alone."

The last word hovered in the air for several seconds until it seemed as isolated and doomed as the man in the bunk. We all remained still, waiting for the man or the word to die. But they were connected now, as if Alf Harley had, out of his semi-comatose state, summarised his condition with one communicable breath. I had never known my father's silence to be so weighted. He was a quiet man, often standing in the stern for hours while fishing, just smoking and gazing at his net curled over the grey waters or sitting in a chair in front of a backyard fire until the embers burned to ash long after everyone in the house and the town had fallen asleep. He was also a man with no significant close relationships outside of his family. But then, men of his generation seemed above friendship somehow. My father's silence wasn't unfriendly; it was just natural for him, easy. Except it wasn't easy as he picked the lantern up by its wire handle and swung it slightly towards me so that the light splashed up to my waist.

"I can take you back now," he said.

Dr. Kaney registered the change as clearly as I did. He frowned, his lips parted, closed, opened again. I shuddered, thinking of the motion of his eyes.

"Harold," he said solemnly, "there's nothing else we can do."

"Alf has always wanted to be left alone."

"In health, yes. In strength."

"Always." My father bent as he stepped towards the wheelhouse.

I scuttled back, almost falling in my haste. Suddenly and inexplicably afraid of being noticed, I withdrew to the deck.

In a matter of seconds, the light and the two men reached me. I saw my father glance at me and hesitate.

"It could be any time," Dr. Kaney said, breathing heavily just from the move from the bow to the deck. "Or a week. I think we need to assume the latter and act accordingly."

My father said nothing.

"I can't come back until the afternoon, at the earliest." The doctor followed my father's gaze, but his expression revealed little. "We should be able to get a party together by then."

Water, perhaps from an earlier rainfall, dripped off the branches somewhere back of us. I looked hard through my breath-clouds to see my father move, but he remained almost perfectly still.

Through this entire conversation, I detected an unsettling lack of authority in the doctor's tone. He seemed to be asking questions even as he made statements. Now, as the silence lengthened, he looked much as he had looked standing in the stern as we approached the island. The invisible dripping water might have been slowly eroding his stillness. I was afraid for him, but I had no idea why. My father, meanwhile, wore an expression I had seen only rarely, after he'd had an argument with my mother – his lips tightened, his jaw was set, and his eyes did not close even to blink.

"I can stay until daylight," Dr. Kaney said. His voice wasn't weak or pleading, but it lacked conviction.

"Nate," my father said, "take the light and go get the thermos and sandwiches."

I hesitated, intuiting that I was being dismissed for my own protection. But from what threat, I couldn't say.

The doctor smiled his disturbingly slow reptilian smile. "It's always coldest before the dawn, as the saying goes. I'm afraid I'm going to need that tea."

Though I knew he meant to reassure me that all was just as it should be, I could still see Alf Harley's open eyes and hear the night's dripping water, now heavy as solder. Almost against my will, I took the shimmering lantern and set off across the wet grasses.

Every minute of the fifteen that I was away, I felt that I'd trapped a hunting owl in my chest. Yet I could not bring myself to hurry either. Speed did not seem a part of the situation since the leaving and the returning seemed exactly the same. I might have started the boat and headed out to sea and that would have been no different than stepping up onto the cedar block, as I did, and finding my father and Dr. Kaney sitting wordlessly in the wheelhouse dark, the red tips of their cigarettes like the eyes of some stalking beast. The tension was as thick as the foul smell rising from the bunk.

The doctor rubbed his hands together as I set the lantern down.

"Ah, just in time. You see that we've chosen the little bit of warmth over the fresh air. But it isn't much warmth. Some tea will help."

My father didn't move except to raise and lower his hand that held the cigarette, so I unscrewed the thermos and poured the slightly steaming tea into the lid.

After taking a sip, Dr. Kaney sighed before subsiding into the fraught silence. Neither thirsty nor hungry myself – but cold to the point of shivering – I kept my hands around the body of the thermos and stared at my father.

The dawn light came slowly on. The men smoked several cigarettes down as their profiles sharpened in the grey air and my hands cooled on the thermos. From outside came the chittering, piercing sounds of life stirring in the rushes. Below us, in the dark bunk, the life stirred intermittently – an infrequent moan, an intake of rattling breath, but never a cry or a word.

At some point in the vigil, I understood that the doctor and my father were arguing without language, but I still did not grasp the nature of the conflict. We were waiting for Alf Harley to die. If he did not die before daylight, my father would take the doctor back to town and, later in the day, a party of men would return to take Alf Harley to the hospital. It was straightforward enough. But the tension was not so easily explained. Yes, I realised that death waited nearby, but this tension had existed before we even reached the island, existed in Dr. Kaney's tired gaze from the deck and my father's first departure with the oil lantern; it existed, too, in the river's tearing of mud from the bank and in the inexorable unseen falling of an old rainfall and the thickening of the dew like silver rust on the tips of the bulrushes.

Apologetically, the doctor, now fully visible, cleared his throat. In his heavy hand, an inch of cigarette trembled. My father turned like an iron weather vane, his eyes as open as the man's in the bunk. I shuddered at the image. And the doctor's trembling climbed up his arm without quite reaching his voice. Firmly but quietly, he said, "I'll just have a last check, then."

My father only nodded.

The doctor lifted his body as if it wasn't part of him. The effort drained even more colour from his face, and now his eyelids didn't even move. He descended to the bunk just like sinking into the marsh.

All I could hear was the beating of my heart. Or perhaps it was my father's heart. I couldn't be certain in the dull, foul closeness of the wheelhouse, but the heartbeats, whosever they were, drowned out the birdsong of first light. My father's unmoving form, however, suggested somehow that his heart had stopped. When he finally raised the lit cigarette to his mouth, I had to look away, for the stick's small fire seemed to be eating my father's face to ash.

Ten minutes later, the doctor rose like Lazarus, grizzle thick as fresh tar on his cheeks, dark as the hollows under his eyes. He did not look at us when he spoke, and yet he was clearly speaking to someone. The words came as slowly and inevitably as the movement of his mouth and eyes.

"The hospital will not be necessary."

My father let his cigarette burn in his hand.

"We will need a party to take him off." The doctor raised his voice a notch. "There are certain protocols." Almost at the taste of the last word in his mouth, he frowned, and his voice softened again. "Of course, there's no great urgency now."

At last, my father stood. He ground his cigarette against the dash, then cupped the crumpled butt in his palm. I shuddered as his flesh closed around the threads of smoke. Somehow, I expected him to take the wheel of Alf Harley's grounded boat and captain it out of the cottonwoods, off the island, off the earth, out of the light of ordinary time altogether. But he did something even more miraculous. He thanked the doctor. It wasn't, however, the common sort of thank you exchanged between men, such as when one fisherman, helping to pull another's net off a snag, shouts "Thanks" over the growl of engines. It wasn't even the sort of thank you that a poor, uneducated man offers a wealthy, well-educated professional for services rendered and improperly compensated for. No, it was a thank you that hardly belonged to the world at all, a thank you stripped of its associations to roles and rules, a thank you that might have come out of any mouth, mine or even the closed mouth under the endlessly open eyes of the dead man in the bunk. I heard it pass by me and echo over the marshes, over the now-changing tide, out to the broad, retreating sea.

The doctor, too, seemed to recognise the rare quality of the words. He almost tried to lean on them. His body, which had returned to his weight and his daily purpose, swayed a little in the fresh eruption of birdsong. I leaned forward myself, eager to hear the words that could follow my father's.

But Dr. Kaney suddenly resumed his place in the order of our town and all towns. He nodded. He bent to his medical bag and picked it up. He smiled his excruciatingly slow lizard's smile, and when he spoke again, it was in the same voice that I heard whenever he finally pulled open the door of the examination room and asked me how my studies were going.

"If you could take me back now, Harold, I can get started on the paperwork."

Within minutes, we had started back across the island, the doctor now in front, as no light was needed, my father a respectful few feet behind him, and myself taking up the rear. Perhaps the order was the order of age, some concession to the natural process of our mortality, and perhaps I was meant to be at the end so I could stop and turn around and imprint the final extinguishing of Alf Harley's smoke on my brain.

But I didn't stop or even look back. All my life lay ahead of me; it was dawn light and birdsong, and even if my dozen years carried an intimation of mortality within them – of Dr. Kaney's death by leukemia and my father's death by kidney failure and of my childhood by the planet's circuiting of the sun – my fate was to advance and not to retreat.

And yet, where was I going that Alf Harley, Dr. Kaney, and my father hadn't already gone? Something followed our leaving across the island, but it wasn't a living creature, nor anything I could easily put a name to. Still, its intensity burned. The tide in the slough made a last desperate swallow. I cast off and anchored in one motion. And though I continued to walk in the way of the world for decades, I already bore my share of the heavy casket on my shoulder, even if youth closed my senses to all the hungers, failures, and urgencies of age, even if the hermit's eyes, within my eyes, hadn't yet opened to erode the hours, one by remarkable one.

The Horses of Darkness

. . .

DRAGGING LONG capes of English rain, the Dutchman, unsettled, prone to bouts of melancholy and ecstasy, finally washed up in the Borinage – a poor and desolate coal-mining region in northern Belgium – intent on immersing himself in his family's other traditional occupation: the ministry. Walking the ash- and soot-blackened road into his assigned village, his gait a little crooked from the weight of his belongings borne in a sack (some clothes, but mostly favourite books – *Hard Times*, *Uncle Tom's Cabin*, a Collected Shakespeare, *The Imitation of Christ*, *Pilgrim's Progress* and, of course, the Bible – and a few of his own sketches), he resembled a large wounded moth that had staggered up from underground into the brightness of day.

Except the day wasn't bright at all. The Dutchman, as was his nature, immediately took in the surrounding tones and shades. Pigeon-grey sky, with snow either just starting or just ending (it wasn't easy to keep the cycles clear); blackthorn hedges that he thought looked, with snow partially covering them, like Gothic lettering on white paper, as in the pages of the Gospel; black ash mounds and brown dung heaps along the road; and, looming ahead of him on the slopes of a long hill, the blacker-than-black chimneys and massive coal piles of the region's oldest mine. Even the wood down in the valley wasn't so black, though the occasional gnarled tree on the roadside showed the most fantastical and inky roots he'd ever seen, like the tentacles of some great sea creature.

The only cheerful colour, in fact, was just beginning to show: the yellow lamplight in the windows of a scattering of miners' huts up on the hillside. Because the Dutchman was meant to billet with one of these miners, as arranged by the Brussels Committee of Church Schools, he lowered his bare head of red hair and forced his stocky body forward.

Within the hour, he had met an emaciated and ghostly pale family, shared their simple and meagre meal of roasted chestnuts, and retreated into his tiny room to recover from his journey and his interminable uncertainty. As the dusk deepened and his candle flame grew brighter minute by minute, he found solace in a way most familiar to him: by writing a letter to his brother. To the sound of the thin and weak children's endless hollow coughing, he moved the blackened nib with his customary speed, as if he was sketching instead of writing. For five feverish minutes, he wrote about his decision to do evangelical work in the Borinage, explaining that he wanted to be of some real use in the world, and what could be better than taking up their father's vocation, but doing so more intensely by following Christ's example?

But just as the words really began to pour out of him, he sensed the shadows in the open doorway. "Yes? What is it?" he said, as patiently as he could.

"We are sorry, monsieur," the worn-out miner's wife said softly. "But the children must go to sleep now."

Only then did the Dutchman notice the other iron cot in the room. He had assumed he would have this tiny space at least to himself, so it was with a frustration that he could not control that he crumpled the paper on which he'd written and threw it to the floor. There will be time for other letters, he told himself, once I have settled into a routine.

"I will just read for five minutes," he said. "If that is all right. Perhaps I should read aloud for the children. Then we will all go to sleep."

The woman, pale as exposed bone, only blinked in response, as if she didn't understand. So, the Dutchman reached into his sack and, pulling out a worn volume, began to read. He stood with his back to the flickering light, and though the words were dim, he had memorised so much of the book that he recited more than he read.

"As the hart panteth after the water brooks, so panteth my soul after thee, O God. My soul thirsteth for God, for the living God: when shall I come and appear before God? My tears have been my meat day and night, while they continually say unto me, where is thy God?"

He finished the psalm, and the next one, before he realised that he had tears upon his cheeks. The children, in one bed, not much more substantial than the limbs of the smoke-blackened and gnarled trees outside, had already entered the redemptive kingdom of sleep. Confident that they would remain there, so clearly exhausted as they were, the Dutchman put the Bible back and removed a cudgel. Lying on his side, naked and crying, he proceeded to beat himself on the shoulders and back. But even this self-mortification was not enough. He rose and, barefoot and thinly covered, left the miner's hut.

The night was cold and star-less, and he immediately began to shiver. The dark was the pure dark of evil, yet he could sense the heavy shift of cloud overhead. It was what he imagined the slow transport of coal blocks underground to be like. Mostly silent, but punctuated with a rumbling like the growl of a great cur. At first, he thought of finding a stable or shack, any simple dwelling in which he could bring himself to the level of suffering of those he sought so desperately to serve. The drip of melting snow and flowing water sounded out of the shadows. Then a horse's rippling neigh. He followed it and soon came to the place of the beasts, where he lay down upon the straw and tasted the thin meat of all his recent days and nights on his tongue.

He had failed at so much. In the family art trade in Paris and London, in the book-selling business, and most recently in his attempts to learn enough Greek and Latin to pass the university entrance exams and train to become a minister like his father. But more than all that – and what tormented him most – he had failed at love. To win it and to give it. And since the latter was more in his power to control, he had chosen to live amongst the poor miners and to help them with their hard lot in life in any way that he could. Believing, with Bunyan and others, that life was a pilgrim's struggling path to the light of God's grace, the Dutchman rushed towards suffering as if it were a long-lost friend, when, in truth, it had been his closest friend, closer than even his beloved younger brother, from the very beginning of his life. Comforted slightly amongst the breathing of cows and horses, he finally drifted off, only to be stunned awake by a terrific crashing and howling that seemed to come from every direction at once.

He rushed out of the stable, away from the crazed whinnying of the horses, just as a crack of yellow light illuminated the landscape for as far as he could see. Thunder tore at the earth and a fierce driving rain almost immediately soaked him to the bone. But even through the water streaming over his eyes, he saw the scene before him with astonishing clarity, looking down from a height to the valley below. Nearest to him, the chimneys and mounds of coal, the miners' huts; and farther off, dark pine woods with white cottages silhouetted against them, a few church spires, the wheel and tower of an old mill. The play of light and dark with each flash of lightning, the thin haze that spread everywhere, put the Dutchman in mind of the pictures of Rembrandt and Ruysdael. But he did not want to think about art. He had not come here for that reason. He had come to serve in his father's way.

The lightning illuminated the landscape once more. He looked to the right and saw with amazement the large gloomy buildings of the coal mine standing isolated in an open field, exactly like the bulk of Noah's ark in the terrible pouring rain and darkness of the Flood. Should he lead the horses and the cattle there? O God, he prayed, tell me what it is that I must do! Listening, he made up his mind, and vowed before he had fallen asleep again that he would act at the earliest opportunity.

. . .

"NO, NO, NO, monsieur, I forbid it. It is a terrible place. A sensitive man like you . . . no, you must not go there."

The Dutchman made no violent protest. He said only, "But I must go, Denis. How can I serve these people if I do not understand their lives? How can I be of any real use to them if I do not know their suffering in all forms? No, one must do like the good God; one must from time to time live among his own. And I have learned already that most of life here is lived below ground."

The baker, a red-complexioned, round-faced man of late middle years, knew there would be no point in arguing further. This Dutchman with the excellent French and the courteous manners was unlike any pastor he had encountered before. Compassionate and generous, yes, but intense and frightening too in his devotion. In the week since he had convinced the new pastor to move to his home, the baker had heard him sobbing at night in his room, had found him on two mornings sleeping almost naked on the bare planks of a shack in the yard (he claimed his room was too luxurious), had seen the evidence of self-inflicted wounds, and had watched the man give away almost all of his clothing and other belongings to the poorest villagers in what seemed a desperate attempt to follow the example of Jesus. But this!

"Then I will come with you. You will not go alone."

The Dutchman smiled and made a slight bow. At the very least, he did have the short, stocky figure of a miner. That would help in the tight places, if he insisted on going there, which the baker suspected he would. He wiped his floury hands on his apron and returned his attention to the large oven. The heat hitting his face made him shudder, for he had known a greater heat and he had long believed that he might be fortunate enough never to know it again.

He looked at the new pastor once more. What a strange fellow he was. Not a very good preacher, it must be said. His words were often halting or else came out in an incomprehensible flood. But he was good at telling Bible stories to the children, and good at tending to the sick. Without question, he had a kind heart, a loving nature. He was particularly fond of animals. The baker had even seen him pick up a caterpillar from the road and place it in the safety of a low branch. Yet there was something about him that made others uneasy. Ah well, the baker concluded, perhaps when he has seen the whole of the miners' lives, he will realise that his mission is futile and will return to Holland and a more comfortable life.

. . .

THE DUTCHMAN HAD not anticipated so much noise. As the spectral group of men and children (some as young as six or seven, including a few girls) trudged barefoot up the hillside in the predawn half light, he could hear a howling and clanking coming out of the mine's main building, as if a suffering beast was trying to escape from chains. But the men and children paid no attention. Bent forward, with their tinned lunches of bread-and-butter sandwiches on strings over their shoulders, they seemed to be looking through the earth to where the next twelve hours would be spent. Despite his faith, which had always given him immense physical courage, the Dutchman was afraid. Given the state of the people he now lived among and meant to serve, how could this underground be anything but Hell?

In a room vast as the nave of a church and illuminated by a handful of smoky lanterns and swimming with shadows, they finally arrived at the mouth of the shaft. The Dutchman, overwhelmed by the machinery – an iron rail with many levers and signals and bars, the joists along which slid two iron cages – hardly had time to take it all in before, in the choking smoke and continual thunder of coal trams being unloaded on a platform, he felt himself swept along, like a small fish in the middle of a school, into one of the cages. He had hardly even noticed that the miners now all carried small lanterns, or that the baker had given him one and shouted to him that he must not wander away out of the light.

Just before the drop began, the Dutchman noticed a large engine thirty metres away, its steel and copper glistening in the dimness. It sat in a raised chamber, on a brick foundation, and a man stood rapt before its flickering signals, appearing to control two massive drums, each five metres around, which rolled and unrolled the two steel cables whose ceaseless rapid motion along a sequence of pulleys was obviously responsible for the raising and lowering of the iron cages. Including the one he stood shivering in now, with forty other humans so like and so unlike himself.

Bells clanged, a loud thumping as of a club against a wooden block never ceased, nor did the indefinable howling. The Dutchman watched the iron cables, whirling so fast they seemed that they must grind to powder. The baker laid a hand on his shoulder. "Prepare yourself," he mouthed over the tumult.

With a violent shudder, followed by a gruesome smoothness, the caged world now truly began. The Dutchman held his breath in the bricky darkness, unsure of whether they fell or rose. His bowels tightened. Everything around him seemed to be flying. For several seconds at a time, the cage made no sound; it just plunged smoothly.

Then all at once there'd come a rough shock which made the cage sway against the shaft's earthen walls. He looked down and saw the naked feet in the yellow lantern light.

A rush of water struck the roof of the cage, falling like rain onto the shoulders of the workers. The Dutchman was soon soaked to the skin with an icy cold. Just then, a flash of light offered a fleeting vision of a cavern full of dark figures. They vanished as quickly as they had come. The baker shouted in his ear. "Only the first level. Three hundred metres. Halfway there."

The rest of the fall seemed to last for hours, though the whole trip, he learned later, had lasted less than a minute. At last, they thudded to a stop, the cage opened, and its occupants stepped out into a chamber cut into the rock and vaulted with masonry. Lit by large lanterns which threw a greasy sheen over the iron flooring, the chamber contained at least four passages heading into the earth in different directions. Trams laden with coal rumbled along the flooring. The Dutchman tried desperately to get his bearings, but his body could not right itself. He leaned against the dripping wall. The fresh smell of saltpetre and – he could hardly believe it – what reminded him of the breath of horses flooded into his nostrils. Raising his lantern, he saw a stable empty of horses, and knew before the thought had even arrived that the human misery wasn't going to be the worst.

Minutes later, the baker led him a little way into one of the chambers, pointing out the wooden scaffolding that was meant to keep the rockface from collapsing onto the workers, who often had to lie on their sides in the same position for hours as they chipped away at the surface with short-handled picks.

"This is far enough," the baker said. "They will walk many kilometres yet. And the passage will become narrower. The water will be at their ankles too. And the heat! Here, you shiver with the cold. That is the air coming from the vents. To keep the air flowing. There..." He pointed at the back of the last miner slipping into the channel like a bee into a hive. "There they will be like the dough in my oven, monsieur. They will be at the Devil's very feet."

"Show me," the Dutchman said. "I need to see it."

Trains of tubs moved along rails near them, and they had to be careful not to get knocked over by one of the several snorting horses that trotted by like phantoms. The icy wind blew in a tempest. The Dutchman couldn't stop thinking about the children's naked feet disappearing into the bowels of the earth.

The baker shrugged. "Only a little further. Not all the way."

Within fifteen minutes, they had to walk doubled over. If not for the leather cap, the Dutchman would have hurt himself badly when his head hit the rocky ceiling. He splashed through the puddles, grimacing, and only the sudden blast of heat in his face distracted him from the pain. Thick floating coal dust weighted his eyelids. A gassy smell threatened to overwhelm him. He gagged soundlessly.

The baker turned and held his flickering lantern out like God's shining hand. "That is enough. We will go back. You see what happens here. Fourteen hours a day, from five or six years. Until death." He spat against the dripping wall. "Which will come too soon. And will be a mercy when it comes. Look here." He pointed to a crevice in the coal face. A slight bubbling escaped from it, as if a songbird was trapped just below the surface. "Put your hand over it. Feel the wind? It's what we call firedamp. Too much of that and there'll be an explosion. Do you wonder, monsieur, why I do not complain about the soot and ash I cannot keep out of my garden or my oven? Do you wonder why a man, put in a cage, grows to resent the pit-man's cry of "Ringing Meat"? It is time to go."

Reluctantly, but not without relief, the Dutchman returned with the baker to the main chamber, where they had to await the next cage for the surface. Exhausted after only an hour of earthly time in this hell, the miners' new pastor did not believe he had compassion enough for the job. But he reprimanded himself immediately. He had long accepted that life was a tortuous path, and whatever torture he had to endure, it was nothing to what Jesus had endured for the sake of his people. Even so, the Dutchman sought comfort by the stables, where a small boy whose skin was a tracing over the bones of his face told him that up to twenty horses lived there. As he spoke, a few horses lifted their heads from munching hay and turned their heads towards the Dutchman, their black eyes wet and gleaming in the lamplight. He had always thought that horse's eyes carried more emotion than human eyes. They looked out at the world with the same sorrow and understanding that perhaps only Christ or Shakespeare could equal.

"And do they ever return to the fields?" he asked.

"Oh no, monsieur," the boy said. "Not until they die."

"But not even when they are too old to work?"

The boy, hearing a rush of sound, jumped off the railing where he'd been seated. "They are never too old. Then they die."

At last, a cage appeared from above. But it moved slowly. The baker explained, "They are lowering a young horse. It sometimes does not go easily. It sometimes even happens that their terror is so great that they are landed dead. This one will have its head bound back to the cage to keep it from flailing about too much."

The Dutchman watched the dark shape, dangling in its net like some great grotesque spider in a web, descend minute by terrible minute. The beast's terrified neighing echoed through the chamber, rising above the thunder of the trams.

"It will never feel the sun again," the Dutchman said. "Or breathe fresh air. Or smell the sun on the grass. Or open its eyes to the dawn. Or gallop across a meadow. Or lie down in moonlight. Or feel the fresh rain on its eyelids. The wind in its mane. Or chew the spring's fresh growth. It will never be what it was meant to be. What God intends it to be."

"Monsieur?" The baker's round face seemed even more round now that his eyes had widened in alarm.

"Or hear birdsong. Crickets. Or see more colours than black and..."

"Are you all right? It has been too much for you. Come. The cage is down."

The Dutchman could hardly bear to see the stunned young horse, unbound from its harness, eyes dilated with terror, lying on its flank, which moved like a bellows, as the animal struggled to adjust to its fate. But the workers waited only a minute before whipping the horse into a standing, quivering position, and finally leading it away.

If I had a knife and the strength, the Dutchman thought, I would put the beast out of its misery. But already he understood that such mercy would come at great cost to the suffering workers and no one else. He understood something else too, but the idea was yet vague and would not take shape for years, after many trials, an outbreak of typhoid, a violent strike in which he would stand up to the bosses on behalf of the miners, great hunger and lost wanderings, even a distancing from his beloved brother who would deem him idle and irresponsible because he would not lead a more conventional life. But the shaping began as soon as he crowded into the iron cage with forty emaciated, damp and shivering miners, all the song in his soul building to a chorus of joy.

The ascent was even swifter than the drop. Soundlessly they flew up through the earth, hurtling towards the light, which, when it came, in a dazzle of shivering yellow, almost blinded him. Stunned by the daylight and God's grace, the Dutchman put his unyoked feet on the path, took up his pencil and his pads, and followed the ringing meat of his own tears to wherever colour would take him.

East and West

. . .

JUST DOWN FROM where the Fraser River divides into its north and middle arms, in what all the fishermen call the main river, the salmon boats would wait their turn to wind a gillnet across a portion of the wide channel, wide enough and deep enough there to accommodate the foreign freighters on their way to load or unload at the New Westminster docks or sometimes even a killer whale chasing a seal to its death.

The fishing was more perilous here, more exciting, and often more productive, than in the quieter side-channels of the south arm where Kyle's father and most of the old-timers liked to work. The tide whipped along with more power, and so did anything carried along with the tide – logs torn off log-booms, for example, or the great lolling stumps of trees like ripped-off heads of monsters. And because the banks were farther apart, it was harder to gauge your position, especially at night. But the salmon usually preferred the deep water and would drive in hard from the Gulf, ferociously bound for the streams and creeks of their birth hundreds of miles inland. As a result, the competition for positioning of boats was often fierce, and no ethnic group could lay claim to the main river as they did for the sloughs. Up here, the Greeks, the Japanese, the Scots, and the Yugoslavs contested the same ground. Most daunting of all, however, was the heavy freighter traffic.

In the middle of the night, in the dense black of those years before Vancouver's power grid gave off its steady orange glow and when the stars still curled like a thousand set cork lines from horizon to horizon, to suddenly see the massive black hull of a freighter, higher than a house, sharp as an orca's fin, bearing down on you was enough to rattle the nerves of even the most seasoned fisherman.

Kyle wasn't seasoned or even close to it, but he was, to use the fisherman's slang, hungry. But not just hungry for fish, for the money they would bring, but also hungry to prove himself. And especially to prove himself in the eyes of his first girlfriend, a thin, soccer-playing fifteen-year-old blonde named Angela whose parents – wealthy professionals who commuted from the south-bank fishing town of Ladner to Vancouver's office towers and who knew nothing about salmon fishing and cared about it even less – thought their daughter was staying the night at a friend's house.

Kyle finished setting the net and looked out into the blackness. He could no longer see the night-light bobbing at the end of his net; all he could see was the twenty lit feet of corks caught in the dull-white glow of his stern-light. He strained to hear sounds above the sound of his own engine. The tide was running out, not yet at full force, but he could hear it slapping the sides of the boat, which lay crossways to the current. A breeze blew in from the southeast, threatening rain. Clouds covered the stars. Kyle smelled gasoline and the briny musk of the salmon he'd caught the set before stiffening in the side-locker beside the drum two feet behind him. He had at least ten minutes before he'd have to pick up, so he called to Angela – who stood on the deck by the cabin – to shut off the engine. She loved to help, so he gave her tasks that wouldn't be too dangerous or complicated, just as his father had given him as a boy.

In the sudden yawning silence, the river seemed to roll over like a great animal, growling and sighing. Kyle swallowed dryly. This was only his second night fishing the main river, and his father and uncle (whose boat he was using for the season) thought he was on one of the calmer drifts in the south arm. They would not have allowed him to fish the main river alone, since he was only seventeen and had never fished by himself until this summer. But if he was careful, and respectful of the other fishermen, and fished only at night when his boat wouldn't be easily recognised, he could make a few sets and possibly out-fish both his father and uncle. There were just more salmon in the main river, and catching salmon was the whole point. Already, he knew that other fishermen scorned the old-timers for their "safe" and largely unproductive drifts, and Kyle wanted to be respected by more than just his relatives.

"Is everything okay?" Angela had stepped into the stern to join him.

He relaxed, seeing her face. It pleased him to know that he could reassure her in this world of fish and boats and men, a world so different from her own family's. But this relaxation didn't last, not even long enough for her to take his free hand (the other clutched the unset part of the net hanging between the drum and rollers).

"Stay here!" he shouted and sprang past her to the cabin. His heart pounding, he turned the key to start the engine and then ran back into the stern.

"What is it? Kyle! What's wrong?"

He hardly saw Angela's face out of the corner of his eye as he stepped on the drum pedal and rapidly began to whir the net in. Five fathoms. Ten fathoms. Terrified, he turned to look over his shoulder. The air itself, black and oily, seemed to plunge forward from the surface of the river to the clouds. A fish dropped out of the tightened web as it lifted to the rollers, but Kyle, hearing the splash, didn't even look. When another fish thumped over the rollers, he didn't stop, but just wrapped it on the drum. Twenty fathoms. Thirty. He could see Angela's hands at her mouth. Was she screaming? He wrapped three more fish on the drum before the rumbling noise of the freighter burst out of the sound of his own engine and the pounding of the blood in his ears.

The black mass, bearing down with its tiny running lights, was now only fifty fathoms off. Kyle swore and jumped on the drum pedal with both feet. As each fathom of net whipped in, his boat pulled a little farther out of the freighter's path. But he knew that avoiding a collision wasn't enough; the wake would almost certainly capsize them, unless his luck held and his net didn't hold a sunken log or his engine didn't conk out.

The rumbling of the freighter's engine filled his ears, a concussive sound that came out of the sky and up from the depths of the river at the same time.

Forty fathoms. Fifty. Angela crouched in a corner of the stern, shrinking with each second. Kyle could hardly see her now. Sweat stung his eyes, and he tried to blink it out. The circle of the dull stern-light shook like water.

As the freighter charged past his bow, Kyle kept frantically pulling the net in. He needed as much distance as possible. Eighty fathoms. A hundred. He'd wrapped twenty fish on before he finally took his foot off the drum pedal and scrambled under the hanging net to grab hold of Angela and pin her to the bottom with his body.

Five terrible suspended seconds passed before the wake struck. They rose and plunged violently down, the boat tipping almost vertically before it reared back the opposite way, nearly throwing them to the other side of the stern. After another minute of rocking, with the sky and the river yoked together and all the loose gear on deck lost to the black waters, the worst appeared to have passed. The freighter's throbbing propeller ground away just above them as the surface of the channel settled slightly, and Kyle began to breathe again. He could hear Angela panting into his chest, could feel her body trembling. The propeller blades seemed to strike him repeatedly as he pulled himself to his feet and assessed the damage.

The stern-light still shook, though the swells were rolling almost gently now, black and glistening, the size and sheen of whale-back. Kyle clutched the taut cork line to steady himself and watched the dark bulk of the freighter slowly pull away. His heartbeats were no longer in his throat, but he quickly began to feel stupid. He should have known better; he should have recognised the warning signs earlier. At the same time, however, he felt a surprising pride. After all, he had faced the danger and survived it; he had protected the boat and the net. Except for a few salmon too damaged to sell and a cooler of sandwiches and pop and an old jacket lost overboard, the damage was minimal.

As he bent to help Angela to her feet, he allowed the exhilaration to flood his veins. No wonder the main river had such a reputation! No wonder his father and uncle wanted to keep him safe in the side channels. Grinning, he looked Angela in the eyes, and saw immediately that she was proud of him.

"That was amazing," she said, her voice as charged as her bold stare. "How did you even know it was coming? I didn't hear anything."

Kyle kissed her, grateful that she didn't blame him or demand to be taken home. And as he kissed her, he wondered how he had known the freighter was there – perhaps he had a pure fisherman's instinct, perhaps next summer he could fish the Gulf and, one year, maybe soon, the north coast or the west coast of Vancouver Island. What had seemed like terror and failure only five minutes before now seemed like a glorious ascension to a new phase of life.

And yet, there was work to be done. Noting that Angela was soaked, he told her to find some dry clothes of his in the cabin. Once she had kissed him again and left the stern, he considered whether he should back the drum up and pick out the mangled salmon (perhaps their flesh would still be saleable) or just keep rolling the net in. Given the increasing speed of the current, which could carry him into more danger if he lingered on the drift, he chose the latter. With both hands on the cork line, he stepped on the drum pedal and the dripping fathoms of mesh began to come over the rollers.

A minute passed. The familiar rhythm of the work settled his nerves. He watched the cork line enter the circle of stern-light at its edge, watching for bobbing or sunken corks that would indicate the presence of a tangled fish. A few more minutes passed. Angela, wearing one of his mack jackets, re-joined him. He could feel her admiration like a second circle of light, a circle that separated them from her parents and their peers and almost the whole world. But Kyle had taken enough from the night's terror to know that he had to concentrate on the light falling on the cork line and the flowing current.

As he did so, something emerged from the frayed darkness that made him take his foot off the pedal and lean forward. He blinked rapidly and ran the back of his forearm across his eyes.

Then the fear hit him, harder than what he'd felt at the freighter's emergence from the dark. For what he saw now wasn't cold and impersonal; it could never be that, whether living or dead. As the net fell slack, the head and shoulders of a man slumped across the cork line and, for a few seconds, remained motionless. Kyle glanced at Angela, but she wasn't watching the net; her eyes lifted to his and she smiled. He looked away quickly, not wanting to frighten her with his own panic. The figure in the net raised itself; the broad face lifted from the water as if the short blond hair of the head had been yanked up by an invisible hand. In the wavering stern-light, Kyle still couldn't be certain if the figure was alive. The night and the current often animated inanimate objects, especially once the imagination joined in.

The engine idled, but Kyle could hear the gurglings of the tide above it. Minute by minute, the river was running out faster to the Gulf – the net had to be brought in. But just as Kyle moved to step onto the drum pedal, the figure cried out, and one arm shot skyward. Angela screamed and threw herself against him, burying her face in his chest. Paralyzed, Kyle gaped at the man in the net, who shouted something in a foreign language easily enough translated by its tone into a cry for help.

There was only one choice to make. Kyle told Angela not to worry, and then he stepped on the drum pedal to bring the man fully into the bright light beneath the rollers.

"Dziekuje," the man gasped. His face was round and flushed with red, but he had sunken dark eyes under a prominent forehead that immediately suggested he wasn't young. As he swam to the side of the boat, where Kyle reached out his hand to help him onboard, the thickness of the man's neck and shoulders, followed by the iron strength of his grip, indicated that he'd spent many years as a worker of some kind.

Once he'd been pulled from the water, he rested on his knees on the side-deck for a minute, coughing and spitting, the water dripping from him as it drips from a dog. Angela, meanwhile, had retreated to the opposite side of the stern, where Kyle joined her, knowing he still needed to tend to the net.

As the drum turned, then stopped while Kyle picked out a salmon or a piece of bark, the stranger slowly got to his feet. Kyle could feel the burning intensity of the man's attention – on the river, on the net, on him, and finally on Angela. But the man neither moved nor spoke. He appeared to recognise the urgency of Kyle's situation – at least he did nothing to get in the way. Kyle would have been grateful for the thoughtfulness if he wasn't still afraid. A corpse in the net might have been better – certainly that wasn't unheard of on the river, as suicides and the drowned, or bodies disposed of for various reasons, occasionally wound up in a fisherman's net. Then the choice was easier: you could get the dead onboard and contact the authorities at the first opportunity, or you could simply untangle the body and let it go (though Kyle couldn't really imagine himself doing so). But a living man – where did he come from? Why was he in the river in the middle of the night? And, most importantly, what would he want? Kyle's heart pounded with the uncertainty as he pulled his bobbing night-light over the rollers, put the engine in gear, and scrambled past the stranger to the deck-wheel, only glancing back into the stern where Angela, wide-eyed and holding her arms around herself, gazed desperately back at him.

Once he'd put the boat on course for the top of the drift, Kyle tried to focus. He knew he had to act. His initial instinct was to head towards another boat, hoping to find someone he knew. But then the fact that he'd been fishing the main river would have been obvious – and gossip was as common among fishermen as gumboots and gaff-hooks. His second instinct was to calm down. After all, the man hadn't done anything threatening; it was just the disturbing manner of his appearance that caused Kyle's nervous system to throb. Even the stranger's mute intensity was probably only the result of his apparent foreignness.

Keeping the throttle low, the boat just creeping up the current, Kyle called out, "Is there somewhere I can take you?"

The figure, clad in black oilskin trousers and a torn, dull orange floater jacket, turned. The large head dropped once, as if it had broken off at the neck, but then lifted immediately. After a few seconds, the stranger, in four broad steps, joined Kyle at the wheel.

"You have cigarette?" he said. But his sunken eyes burned into the darkness, scanning the banks of the silt islands.

Kyle didn't smoke, but his uncle did. "Just a minute." He ducked into the cabin, found a pack of cigarettes and some matches, and brought them back to the stranger.

"Dziekuje... dank you," he said, and struck a match off his front tooth. His first inhale shrank the stick almost by half. He exhaled at length through his nostrils. Kyle could hear the man's thoughts grinding away under the sound of the engine, and he realised at once the danger he was in. The man was not taller than Kyle – about five foot eight – but he was squat and thick, and there was no question that the arms under the jacket were as powerful as the shoulders' width promised.

"No one lives on island?" he asked.

Kyle followed the direction of the man's gaze, while noting that he pocketed the pack of cigarettes.

"No. There are no people there." In fact, only a few of the islands in the estuary – and only the largest one this far towards the mouth – were inhabited.

The stranger nodded and took another long drag on the cigarette. After exhaling, he suddenly announced, "Janisch," and held out his hand. "Polski," he added, as he and Kyle completed a firm handshake. "My ship." He pointed upriver towards the blackness into which the freighter had vanished. "I leave. I not go back. I stay." He seemed to be talking to himself, especially as he followed these words with a string of what Kyle took to be Polish. "You take me there? To island?"

Kyle was relieved and confused at the same time. He could easily drop the man off on one of the little islands, but he didn't understand why he should want to go there instead of to the mainland. There wouldn't even be any shelter, other than trees. Kyle, with caution, studied the stranger more carefully.

His face was huge and the cheeks a marbled red and white, but from the jaw line down a dark grizzle seemed to keep his head from floating off, like sand in the bottom of a balloon. The mouth was almost lipless – just a thin line – but when he opened it, the number of large, crooked teeth made a shocking contrast. It was as if he was continually chewing a mouthful of bones.

"Sure," Kyle finally said, "I can take you there." But then curiosity overcame caution. "Why?"

Now the Pole turned his full concentration on Kyle instead of the river and the bank of the approaching island. He seemed to be sizing him up. Kyle repressed a shudder and looked away, his gaze falling on Angela in the stern. Guiltily – because he had almost forgotten her – he gave her a thumbs-up. But she appeared to be frozen in place.

"I defect," the Pole suddenly announced. "I stay this country. You will help, yes? You a good boy. You help Janisch."

Now Kyle realised he was even more out of his depth than he thought. Of course, he knew from social studies classes at school that Poland was a communist country; and he knew about the Cold War; he even knew, mostly because of the Olympics, that people from Communist countries sometimes defected to the west. But he knew nothing about the legalities involved. Could a defector stay in Canada just because he wanted to? Probably not, otherwise the Pole wouldn't have risked jumping off his ship at night. And he certainly wouldn't want to be taken to an uninhabited island.

As Kyle steered closer to an open section of muddy bank, he began to panic. What if helping a defector got him into trouble? What if the government or the RCMP confiscated his uncle's boat? What if he – or even worse, his uncle or father – had their fishing licences taken away?

The questions must have been written all over his face because Kyle felt the Pole's concentration like an electric jolt.

"I have Canadian money," he said. "For food." Obviously frustrated, he began to speak in Polish and to make hand gestures, none of which Kyle could interpret. All he could understand was the man's desperation.

"You bring to me bread on island. And drink. Meat. Next day." The bones shifted in his mouth. His face reddened and lifted from his thick neck. "Big trouble for me. You tell no one. Our . . . what is word?"

"Secret," Kyle said, barely above a whisper.

The Pole nodded rapidly. "Ja. Secret. Is good. Tell no one. We brothers, yes?" And he laid a heavy hand on Kyle's shoulder.

Kyle put the boat in neutral and turned it sideways to the bank.

"Clothes," the Pole said. "You have?"

Quickly, Kyle bent into the cabin and grabbed a spare jacket and shirt. Returning, he found the Pole already on the bank, a foot above deck height. The man held his arms out and Kyle handed him the clothes. As the current pulled the boat away and the Pole dissolved into the darkness, Kyle caught a last glimpse of him gazing intently back, the clothes like a limp body in his arms.

A moment later, Angela stood beside him on the deck, full of questions that he couldn't adequately answer. But because she was a better student than him, from a family who followed world events, she had an explanation for the Pole's desperate actions.

"I don't know much about it, but things are worse there now. I think there's been more defections." Visibly, her whole body trembled as she looked at the island. "We ought to help him. But... he's not... there's something scary about him. Whenever he looked at me..."

Kyle nodded, knowing exactly what she meant. He wasn't sure that helping the Pole was a good idea. And yet, he couldn't just abandon him on the island either; he'd have to bring him some supplies at least. After all, he'd promised, or rather he hadn't said that he wouldn't, which amounted to the same thing. Maybe he could find a way to get some advice without providing too much information, especially without revealing that he'd been fishing the main river without permission.

At any rate, he'd had more than enough excitement for one night. Turning the bow downriver with the current, he steered for one of the quiet side-channels with considerable relief. He needed to clear his net of bruised fish, and he needed time to breathe and think things through before setting his net for the daybreak set.

Two hours later, with Angela sleeping in the cabin, Kyle stood in the stern, shivering as the first pale tinge of light seeped out from behind the mountains. He watched the cork line for action but saw nothing except the Pole's still body on the receding bank of the island. He felt that he should stop fishing immediately and go into town for supplies; he felt that both his father and uncle, had they known of the situation, would have made the stranger's plight their top priority. And yet, somehow Kyle couldn't face up to the task. Whenever he imagined approaching the island, walking across its marshy flatness to the poplars, finding the Pole and, thereby, deepening his involvement with him, his stomach tightened. It wasn't just the fear that helping the stranger might lead to serious trouble; it was also something in the Pole's desperation. Kyle knew, without being able to analyse the knowledge, that the Pole had violently yoked another world – a darker, fiercer, uglier one – to his world. Thinking about the man's great head with its mouth full of chewed bones kept Kyle sharply awake through the whole numbing hour of the first dawn chill.

When fishing closed later that morning, and he delivered his catch to the packer and returned to town, Kyle found that the Pole's ugliness had grown so large in his imagination that he was relieved to be off the river, as if by walking down streets of houses he was putting oceans between himself and the stranger's desperate need.

In the harbour, as they moored the boat, Angela asked what he planned to do. Kyle only shrugged.

A day later, she dropped by his house, and eventually the subject came up again.

"I read in the paper," she said, "that things are really terrible in Poland. I'll bet he's really worried about his family."

"How do you know he has any family?" Kyle busied himself with filling a hanging-needle and did not look at her.

"Everybody has family." Angela's voice grew quiet. "Kyle? You are going to help him, aren't you?"

He didn't raise his head. "Sure. I'm going to help him. But not everybody has family. He didn't mention any. Maybe he decided to defect because he's all alone."

"Can I go with you when you take him some food?"

Now Kyle did look up, quickly. "Why?"

She seemed startled by his vehemence. "It's just interesting, that's all. I mean, we're the only ones who know he's there." She chewed her lower lip for a few seconds. "I guess they know he's gone by now."

"Who knows?"

"On his ship. The captain and rest of the crew. They'll know he's defected."

"I suppose so." Kyle's hands started to shake as he wound the twine on the needle.

"So, I can go with you?"

"Sure," he said quietly, still avoiding her eyes. "I'll call you when I get the stuff together."

. . .

BUT WHEN KYLE called Angela a few days later, he lied and said that he'd gone back to the island with food and clothes but that the Pole was gone.

"I walked all over, through the woods, calling out. But he wasn't there. I guess he got someone else to take him off. Or maybe he swam to the mainland. That's easy enough if the tide's slack."

Kyle knew from her hesitation and then the tone of her voice that she didn't believe him. "Really? It seemed like he trusted us, that he was counting on us to come back."

"Yeah. I was surprised he wasn't there."

Then all the pretending stopped.

"Kyle! You didn't go, you didn't take him any food!"

"Of course I did. And I left it there too, in a cooler, just in case."

"I know you didn't. How could you do that? He's all alone. He's probably terrified. He's probably watching for your boat every minute."

As soon as Kyle imagined the Pole's face gazing out over the water looking for him, he realised that he was never going back to the island, no matter what Angela thought.

"Well, I told you he wasn't there. It's not my problem if you don't believe me."

"I have to tell my dad. He'll know what to do."

Panic rose in Kyle's throat. "If you tell your dad, I'll tell him you were with me all night. I'll tell him you've been fishing the main river with me."

Angela was silent for a few seconds. "Then your dad and uncle will know too."

Suddenly, Kyle realised that the Pole had already cost him one of the most important relationships in his life and was threatening the others. But the realisation only made him anxious to have nothing to do with the Pole ever again. If he starved on the island, Kyle didn't care. He hadn't asked for some foreign country's problems to swim into his net in the middle of the night; he wasn't old enough to be fishing the main river anyway, so how could he be expected to deal with some desperate man more than twice his age?

"I don't care what you do," Kyle said. "It's your word against mine."

Now the hurt came into Angela's voice. "Kyle? He's a human being. You can't just abandon him."

"I told you. I took him some food and he wasn't there. I waited for over an hour. What else am I supposed to do?"

And then the phone clicked, and one day ran into the next, and Kyle never heard from Angela or her father or anyone else about the Polish defector. When Kyle returned to fishing, he avoided the main river, and, in fact, stayed as far away from the Pole's island as possible. Eventually, since he never heard anything more about the stranger, he assumed that he'd gotten off the island somehow and just vanished into the city or maybe even deeper into the continent. By the time the fishing season ended and Kyle was back at school for his final year, he had stopped thinking about the Pole. He got a new girlfriend, started working at a grocery store, and then, the next summer, decided to drive a combine in the pea fields instead of fishing his uncle's boat. After that, the years accumulated; he changed jobs and girlfriends a few times, eventually got married, fathered a couple of kids, moved to Ontario where his wife was from.

. . .

I SAW HIM last week, about thirty years after his big night on the main river. He'd returned to our hometown for his uncle's funeral, and I happened to run into him at the pub down by the harbour. He was a little drunk at the time, probably to help forget about his uncle's death, and after another round, he became downright conversational. We got to discussing how much the coast had changed, how sad the loss of the fishery was, how there were hardly any old-timers left.

"Looks like we're the old-timers now," he said. And then, after a long pause, he asked if I'd ever fished the main river.

"A few times," I said. "A bit too fast for my liking."

And that was when he told me about the Pole. I guess he wanted some kind of reaction from me, but when I didn't offer one, he seemed almost relieved, as if he figured I'd blame him somehow. After a half-minute, he looked up from his almost-empty glass.

"The funny thing is, I didn't think about that night again until a year or so ago. You'd figure a guy would think a lot more about something like that. But I guess I felt guilty, kind of blocked it out, I don't know. It just seemed easier to forget about it."

He motioned to the server for another beer, then turned a sad smile on me.

"But now I can't *stop* thinking about it. About him, I mean. I even made a trip out here last summer and borrowed my cousin's boat and went walking around on the island. Don't know what I expected to find. Some bones maybe." He grinned but somehow didn't seem amused. "But the weird thing was, I could feel him staring at me, standing there with those clothes in his arms, watching me leave as if he already knew I wasn't coming back and that he'd have to make other plans. I could have sworn he was still on the island. An old man, like that fellow in the book."

"Robinson Crusoe."

"Yeah, that's the one. Of course, there wasn't anybody there. But the Pole – Janisch, I should call him, since we were brothers, after all..." – He mockingly put his wrists together – "is probably still alive somewhere. And if he is, he could be thinking about that night too."

I didn't know what he was driving at, but he was too drunk by then to notice my reaction.

"And I hate the thought of him thinking about me just as much as I hated him staring at me all those years ago. Isn't that weird? It's like I have to spend the rest of my life stuck to someone I turned my back on when I was just a kid."

His own words seemed to startle him.

"Well, I didn't exactly turn my back. I never said I'd bring him any food. Least I'm pretty sure I didn't. The thing is..." His face swam towards me. "My kids are almost adults now, and... well, the world's not very fucking friendly, is it? Whenever I think about that night, it pisses me off more than ever. Why didn't he just stay on his ship and go back to his own country? Why do they have to bring all their problems over here?"

"It's a small planet," I ventured, glancing at the red exit sign.

He nodded, and the aggression drained from his body. "Whenever I think of him, it's like he's one of my own kids. You see? That's the problem. He's out there, maybe thinking about me, maybe not, but at any second he's going to jump again and need somebody's help and . . ." He rubbed his face with the palms of both hands. "Seems like that's the world. Either you jump, or you have to deal with the jumpers. Either way, it's a shit show."

Normally, I would have smiled to hear the colloquialism of the lost river culture, but I have kids too, and what he said suddenly seemed to turn everyone in the pub into refugees, their dark bodies drifting on some invisible tide towards other dark bodies, the whole mass of human flesh exiled and bearing down, without lights, on a future desperate to get out of the way.

I left him then, gazing into the bottom of his glass as if it contained all the dark dregs of history, but of course I couldn't really leave him.

Outside, for a good ten minutes, I sat in my car with the headlights on, thinking about what he'd told me, trying to remember if there was someone out there who might be thinking of my young and frightened self. For a terrifying few seconds, I almost saw a face swim out of the dark into the beams of light, but then I wisely reversed the car and the straining image drifted away.

Tidal Change

. . .

THE GREAT BLUE heron had been standing on one skinny leg for twenty minutes when the first human thought entered his brain. He did not shift position out of an instinct, or out of some glittery stimulus in the muddy shallow waters of the salt marsh; he unfolded his heavy wings and lifted one leg as he placed the other down simply because it occurred to him that he could. No one was going to stop him. At this moment, he did not have enough familiarity with human thought to create the kind of language that would lead to the term "free will," but everything was happening very rapidly. The dark clouds scudding just above the rippling poplars and cottonwoods had all the speed of prey. The heron reared up, prepared to lunge with his bill at the sky, and then caught himself. This was the second human thought – doubt following upon boredom – and now the transformation was occurring so quickly that the bird raised a dripping pale-blue wing to his narrow question-mark of a skull, as if to protect himself from a barrage of ideas and words.

But it was too late. The wing was already an arm and a hand, and the skull had thickened and broadened and developed a jaw, cheekbones, and a furrowed brow. By the time the hand had touched the brow, the heron had grown to six feet tall; he had chest, torso, legs, and a strange new blood coursing through his veins. His long feathers turned into a worn woollen sweater and ripped blue jeans, his crown became a sodden toque, his throat plumage a grizzled beard. Only his eyes remained similar: small and red and intense. He fixed them now on the small town across the river, a sleepy place of rain-darkened shops and grey streets all potholes and oil-splatters. And as he climbed the bank and his bare feet touched the earthen path through the blackberry bushes, a new word came to him. Thirst.

Ten minutes later, without knowing how or even why, the great blue heron entered a small brown building listing in the rain-slant and took a moon-round seat at a shining wood counter stained with the rings from glasses. His feet were sore, bloodied a little from the sharp pebbles along the roads, and rain glistened in his beard and trickled down his sunken cheeks.

A young man with a shaved head approached on the other side of the counter. He had a large hoop earring in one ear and multiple tattoos on his forearms and neck. The heron almost remembered the patterns on the skin of certain snakes he used to eat, but all of that was vague now, much less vivid than his desire to appease his thirst. The tattooed man said, "Yeah? What'll it be?" And now the heron experienced fear. He had not spoken in this new body. And the thought came to him that if he opened his mouth and emitted a long, harsh croak, he would somehow be in trouble. So when the tattooed man suggested, "Beer?", the heron nodded, his red eyes darting to the mirror high on the wall behind the counter. In that silvery glass, he saw the room behind him: two men playing pool, several empty tables and chairs, two women, neither young nor old, at one table, leaning close together and whispering. The heron did not understand why, but he was so interested in the one woman that, when his drink came, he turned sideways on his seat to get a clearer view of her.

She had a round, very pale face, painted thickly around the eyes, and a small, moist mouth out of which the pink tip of her tongue kept emerging. Her breasts were large and strained against an aqua-green T-shirt. She smoked a cigarette. And the way she withdrew the tip of her tongue to insert the end of the cigarette excited the heron. His hardness startled him so much that he spilled a little of his beer, and the tattooed man narrowed his eyes at him from over the taps. The heron drank, only a sip at first, then a long swallow. He had never tasted water like this, but by the time he had finished his glass and nodded for another, the drink was an old familiar and his whole self cozied up to it. He sighed. He shifted to make his hardness more comfortable. And now he recognised – though it wasn't a thought so much as a different kind of instinct – that the woman was stealing glances at him and only half-listening to her friend. The heron told himself to be patient.

And while he waited, he started to remember. Memory was so new to him that he could not tell if the rain and the river and the rising and falling of the tides derived from his old life or from the one he was living now. Either way, he tasted salt and saw the moon's fullness and understood that these were connected to the movement of fish, and that the movement of fish was connected to time. He looked into his hand that did not hold the glass of beer. The skin was heavily lined, scarred in a few places, and felt heavy. The word and the idea of time felt heavy too. But the taste of the alcohol fought that heaviness. As he put his lips to the cold rim of the glass, the woman rose from the table and walked towards him.

Now memory ran fast the other way. He could see a whole world unfolding: first, the rich waters of this woman's body under his touch, then the alleviation of that bitterness in the salt taste, and then its return, far off on the horizon. The image chilled him, but the warmth of her voice and the scent of her skin beneath the cigarette smoke lifted the chill.

"I see you got caught in the rain," she said. And then, with a sad look that, again by instinct, he leaned towards as if to strike, she added, "What happened to your feet?"

The heron understood that the salt taste, like the taste of the beer, was the anticipation of pleasure and possibly also pain, and the knowledge gave him the courage to speak. And while his voice was low and gravelly, it did not betray him. The thought of betrayal, though, completed the first phase of the transformation as he watched the woman's tongue and the darkness between her breasts and the murky bottom of his third and fourth glasses.

. . .

TWO YEARS PASSED. The heron lived with the woman in a float home at the edge of the estuary, almost where the river merged with the ocean. The movements of fish still directed his life, for he worked as a fisherman in the summer and fall months, using nylon nets stretched across the tide to snare the salmon's flexed muscle. And though he often considered the moon and the wind and the tides, they were no longer as much a part of him as his own breath and blood. At first, he had felt the difference, but no longer. Now he was aware only of a curious emotion and a new word – loneliness. It was not a crippling emotion, nor did he experience it all the time. Usually, when he held the woman in his arms, or even when he just thought of her, the loneliness abated. But out on the river, just before daybreak, in that pearl-pale light when the great blue herons rose from the tall rushes and dragged the creaking chains of their hunger towards the tidal flats, he felt a hard pang in his chest that drove him to the cooler with the beer in it. Sometimes, by mid-morning, he was drunk and the multicoloured corks on his cork line blurred and he always dropped a few salmon from the net into the river when he was bringing in the catch.

He kept to himself, except for the woman. She chided him for not wanting to go out more and to be around people, but she was solitary herself by nature, prone to dark moods and bouts of drinking, and so they were mostly content to suffer one another's behaviour. Overall, their lives had fallen into a regular, if not always smooth, rhythm. The heron, though he could use human language comfortably, preferred silence, and since the woman seemed to find that quality in him particularly attractive, they lived with more silence than most couples.

By this time, the heron was fully a man; he retained only a vague awareness of the lives of other species, and he understood that there were times when being a man meant a terrible and strange separation, not only from other men and even the woman whose bed he shared, but also from himself. There were occasions when he hurt the woman with his silence or his desire for solitude, and he knew he was hurting her and yet did not stop. Strangest of all, he knew that this was really a way of hurting himself. Yet he still could not stop. It seemed to him, at his most sober, lucid moments, that a change must come. When it did, he was not even remotely prepared for the form it took.

"I'm pregnant," the woman said one night as she stood at the kitchen sink washing dishes. Her voice had a curious, low quality, at once tender, afraid, and awed. When he didn't respond, she continued, turning her tear-streaked face to him, "I never thought I would be. I didn't think it could happen, not after so long..."

The man who had been a heron saw that she wanted his love now, more than she'd ever wanted it, but his breath came quick and shallow, and he refused to take her in his arms. Pregnant. He knew the word, knew that it was related to the word "miscarriage," a loss the woman had suffered decades before when she was very young.

"I'll be forty," she said quietly. "Quite a birthday present."

Still, he did not relax his body and step towards her. He did not even understand why. But the idea of becoming a father made him almost physically ill. Out of desperate kindness, he tried to hide his condition from her. He lifted his forearm to cover his eyes, and the woman reached out and gingerly touched it.

"When did you get this done?"

She turned his forearm over. A small, pale-blue stain in the shape of a crescent moon and constellations covered an inch of the skin. He had not noticed the stain before, but he intuited that he must hide the fact of his ignorance. He said that he'd had it done a few days earlier, in a pub in a town across the river. It was just an impulse, he explained, and forced a smile. But it worried him that he could not remember getting a tattoo, that he had been so drunk that he couldn't even recall wanting to get one. Blackout. He knew that word too. But somehow that explanation was inadequate. Tattoos had never interested him.

The woman frowned. "You must have been drunk." And in her words shone the clear statement: now that I am with child, your drinking must stop.

He heard it and he clenched his fists hard at his sides. When he did so, his fingers did not quite close as usual. A little triangle of thin skin appeared between each finger and its neighbour, at the base. He turned his head sharply, as if at a cry from the river through the open window.

The woman's shoulders shook violently. "You're not pleased," she said. "You don't want this."

But the man hardly took in her words. He felt dizzy. The brine on the air startled him with its heaviness, the river suddenly ran hard and cold against his thighs. He put his arms out to maintain his balance and the flash of pale blue along the skin forced a harsh gasp from his throat. The woman screamed. He looked wildly at her. She grew monstrous and he struck at her to get away, but his arms had changed. Now the river was like a storm in his senses, his vision suddenly intensified, he threw himself hard against the kitchen wall. Where was the moon? What was the wind saying? He flung himself at the ceiling and struck it and cried out hoarsely above the woman's piercing screams. But even in his terror, as he was forgetting everything he had been for the past two years, all the embraces and the words and the pain that was so much like pleasure, he saw the woman's pain and her loneliness and the suffering that she would know, the fear over the life she carried inside her, and one final human thing – one tear – fell from his red eye and slid off his long bill and broke on the woman's bowed head.

She did not respond to it, and seconds later the heron had found the open window and forced his body through the narrow space, returned forever to the hard flight and the stillness and the killing lunge at life.

As a boy, Tim Bowling liked to pose in front of his brother Bruce's Valiant and dream about one day publishing a collection of short stories. Fifty-five years later, his dream has come true! The author of twenty-four other works of poetry and prose, and a recipient of many honours (including five Alberta Book Awards and a Guggenheim Fellowship), Bowling grew up at the mouth of the Fraser River and now lives close to the banks of the North Saskatchewan River.

Acknowledgements

. . .

SEVERAL OF THESE stories previously appeared in the following publications:

Fiddlehead, *The New Quarterly*, *Alberta Views*, *Grain*, *Queen's Quarterly*

I wish to thank the Canada Council for the Arts, the Alberta Foundation for the Arts, and the Edmonton Arts Council for financial assistance.

My gratitude to Deborah Willis for her incisive and motivating editorial suggestions, and to Kelsey Attard and everyone at Freehand Books for their enthusiasm, expertise, and support.

Thank you to Noelle Allen for permission to reuse in altered form a small section from *The Call of the Red-Winged Blackbird* (Wolsak and Wynn, 2022).

Indispensable assistance of varying kinds has come from Paul Vermeersch, Peter Cocking, Jean-Marcel Morlat, Joan Harcourt, Nola Bowling, the Amazing Mr. Hugo, Marco Melfi, Norm Sacuta, Rick and Pat Bowling, Jay Peterson, Jackie Baker, Bruce and Flo Bowling, Chris Wiesenthal, Dave Stadel, Russell Thornton, and Theresa Shea.